Tom Gates is ABSOLUTELY FANTASTIC

(at some things)

By Liz Pichon

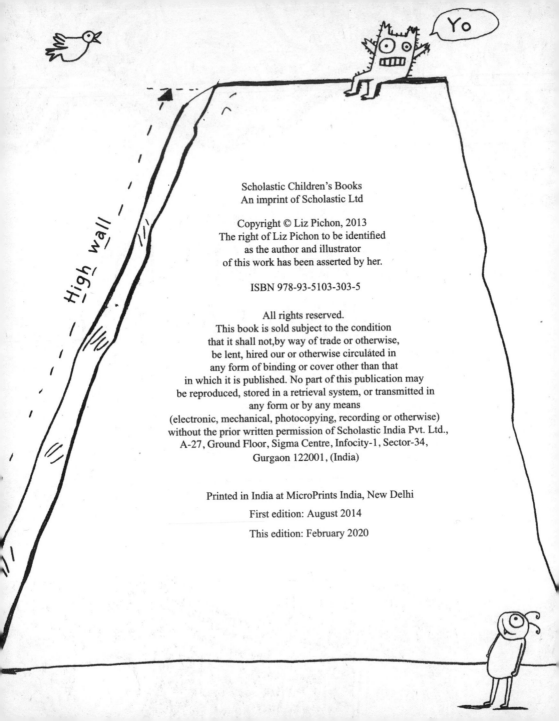

Scholastic Children's Books
An imprint of Scholastic Ltd

Copyright © Liz Pichon, 2013
The right of Liz Pichon to be identified
as the author and illustrator
of this work has been asserted by her.

ISBN 978-93-5103-303-5

Printed in India at MicroPrints India, New Delhi

First edition: August 2014

This edition: February 2020

High wall

Yo

For my lovely mum,

Joan

From your
(not always so)
lovely daughter

Liz xx
xxx

Remember
Bug-eyed
bear?
I still have him – he
looks like Mr Fullerman

To Team
Scholastic

MASSIVE
thanks to
EVERYONE at
Scholastic for
all the hard work
you put into the
books – I am
VERY grateful
Love Liz xx

I WISH school started at **eleven o'clock** in the morning and **NOT** at quarter to **nine**

Groan

(which is far too early for me).
I'm RUBBISH at getting up on time.

It takes me **AGES** to get my brain working and even longer for my  eyes to open.

Mr Fullerman (my teacher) is
ALWAYS WIDE AWAKE.

Right now he's at the front of the class, being all **BUSY** and LIVELY while writing random words on the board that don't make any sense at all.

He says,

"You're probably wondering why I'm writing all these words down."

(Er, slightly.)

"Does anyone want to ADD their own interesting word to this list?"

(I keep quiet.)

Then someone at the back of the classroom says, CAKE, sir. Which is a good choice (everyone likes cake, don't they?).

Mr Fullerman writes "CAKE" on the board.

Then Mark Clump suggests BUG and Julia Morton wants PENCIL (which is NOT that interesting, but Mr Fullerman writes it down anyway). ALL the time I'm thinking to myself – I wonder WHY Mr Fullerman never ever seems to look tired?

4

MAYBE it's because his EYES are

so MASSIVE and

WIDE and STAREY?

Mr Fullerman really does have the

MOST
ENORMOUS
BIG
 ←BEADY
EYES.

That's what I'm thinking.

Only I'm <u>NOT</u> thinking it.

I'm actually SAYING IT -

OUT LOUD.

"BIG
BEADY EYES."

"I'm sorry, Tom, did you say something?"

Mr Fullerman is staring  right at me.

 "No, sir."

"It sounded like you said BIG BEADY EYES, Tom?"

 (Think ... think...) "No, sir."

"What was it you said, then?"

"I said ... BIG MEATY PIES, sir."

Which makes everyone in the class LAUGH Ha! Ha! Ha!

(apart from me).

7

Mr Fullerman gives me another L⊙⊙K
and says,

"That's THREE words, Tom – choose | one. |"

I PANIC and say ➡ PIES,

which he writes down on the board.

Mr Fullerman explains what he wants us to
do next.

**"I'd like you all to write a short story that
includes as MANY of these WORDS on the
board as you can.**

Your story can be about anything you want. So get creative!"

Great ... if I'd known THAT, I would have picked a slightly more useful word to use in a story, like IT or AND.

Definitely not PIEs.

Once upon a ~~PIE~~.

~~There was a BIG PIE.~~

LIST OF WORDS

STORMY

 GIGANTIC

  RUNNING

   SURPRISED

    CAKE

     NICE

      SMALL

       BUG

        PENCIL

         FRIDGE

          PIES

(Mr Fullerman didn't say the story had to
make any sense, which is just as well, really –
here goes.)

ENGLISH

MY SHORT STORY By Tom Gates

It was a STORMY night when I SURPRISED my grumpy sister Delia by RUNNING her a GIGANTIC bath. She was very happy until I pointed out there was a BUG sitting on her head. I suggested she could wash it off in the bath. But Delia got cross and tried to *flick* it away with a PENCIL instead.

Eventually when she went off to have her bath, I helped myself to the delicious PIES that were in the FRIDGE. There was CAKE too. I ate most of it. But because I am a NICE brother, I left Delia a really SMALL piece. (Here it is.) ➡ The end.

There - all done.

O nce I've finished my story, my mind → 🙂

turns to other things, like **DOGZOMBIES**

(which is the name of my and Derek's band).

I decide to experiment by drawing ✏️

a few different types of d**o**g**s**

as **ZOMBIES** for a change.

Usually I draw them like this.

Grrrrr

But today I think I'll draw a new one, then a

HUGE dogzombie,

a bonkers dogzombie,

a tiny dogzombie,

a sausage dogzombie...

I'm just getting started when Mr Fullerman STOPS my drawing completely...

But today I think I'll draw a new one

a tiny
dogzombie,

a sausag
dog.

I'm just getting starte

STOPS my drawing compl

"TOM – as you've OBVIOUSLY finished your story and have found time for drawing, you can hand out the NEW school planners to the class."

"YES, sir."

...Sigh.

Marcus Meldrew  (who sits next to me) is very IMPATIENT. He sees the new planners and tries to SNATCH one from the pile.

"Give me MY planner, Tom ... hand it over."

Which is a bit rude.

So I say, "Calm down, Marcus, you'll get yours eventually."

Then I take a planner from the top of the pile and pass it over his head right round to AMY PORTER.

Whoops

"Here we go, AMY - your planner."

This winds Marcus up. He tells me, "Hurry up, I WANT my planner NOW!"

He's tugging at my jumper, which is annoying. So I ignore him and begin giving out the planners from the BACK of the class, working my way to the front.

By the time I reach Marcus, he's practically tearing his hair out with frustration.

"Last but not least - your planner."

Marcus goes to GRAB it from me and Mr Fullerman says,

"Don't snatch, Marcus."

I agree - so I hand Marcus his planner in

EXTRA s l o w m o t i o n.

(Which is funny and makes Marcus more

CROSS  - a double whammy.)

Mr Fullerman says that if we've finished our stories (like me ☺) we should write our names on the planners, then take a GOOD löök through them and REMIND ourselves of any **SPECIAL SCHOOL EVENTS** that are coming up this term.

"These planners are for you to write down **IMPORTANT** information. Like when your homework is due in."

(Which is not *my* idea of important information.)

I'm flicking through the first few pages of the planner. There's the usual school stuff inside like:

Oakfield School Behaviour Policy
(I didn't even know we had one.)
A calendar
School holiday dates ☺
(VERY important.)

Dates for school reports (:(Not so important.)

School fairs

Sports days

School photographs – blah

blah blah.

There are also a few blank pages for <u>NOTES</u>.

I cross out ~~NOTES~~ and write

 instead. Then I spot

something that I'd completely forgotten about

marked VERY clearly:

Special Events

YEAR FIVE – School Activity Trip

MONDAY

TUESDAY

| WEDNESDAY |

WHICH IS BRILLIANT NEWS!

I nudge **AMY** and

say, "HEY, I'd forgotten about

the **SCHOOL ACTIVITY TRIP!** That's good,

isn't it?" and she says,

 "Haven't you put your name down
already?"

And I say "NO."

"Didn't you get the letter
WEEKS ago about the trip?"

"Er, NO?"

"So I'm guessing your
parents didn't fill in the form or go

to the meeting about the trip either?"

"**No and no**," I say.

THIS is not sounding promising at all.

Then <u>just</u> when I think things can't get any worse, Marcus joins in the conversation.

"You won't be going then, Tom. It's fully booked up now. Bad luck."

HOW DID THIS HAPPEN?

I'm trying to remember what I did with the VERY important **SCHOOL ACTIVITY TRIP LETTER?**

Think think

OK, just remembered.

AMY must think I'm some kind of idiot losing my letter (well, sort of losing it) – groan.

I tell her, "I'm not normally so forgetful."

"Yes you are, Tom," **AMY** says.

(Which is a bit TRUE.)

If I don't get to go on the trip, I'll be missing GOOD stuff like:

☺ climbing (I'm not bad at that)

☺ Swimming (good)

☺ Kayaking (which is a kind of canoeing I've never done before – sounds good)

☺ Building STUFF (can't wait)

Every year the kids who've been on the trip ALWAYS come back and tell EVERYONE how FANTASTIC it was.

(Which can be a bit annoying.)

The trip was AMAZING! BRILLIANT! So good!

I really want to go. Sigh

AMY suggests I talk to **M**r Fullerman about getting another form. Good thinking. ☺ I put my hand up and say,

Mr Fullerman, I've just seen the **SCHOOL ACTIVITY TRIP** in my planner – is it too late to put my name down?

Mr Fullerman looks at me from his desk and says, **"I hope not, Tom. I'll give you another letter. Try not to lose this one, will you?"**

(How did he know I'd lost it?)

When I see my best mate Derek at break time, I ask him about the SCHOOL ACTIVITY TRIP. He says, "I thought you were going?" I say, "No, I forgot, and now it might be too late."

Derek says, "It won't be as much *FUN* * without you, Tom."

Which is nice of him, but doesn't help my situation. EVERYONE seems to be going - apart from me.

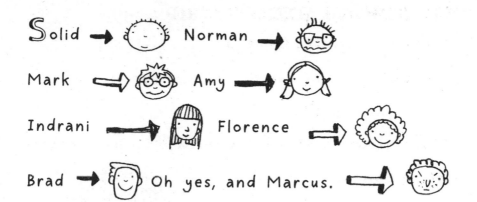

Solid → Norman →
Mark ⇒ Amy →
Indrani → Florence ⇒
Brad → Oh yes, and Marcus. ⇒

Every time I 👁 👁 see Marcus, he doesn't stop reminding me that HE'S GOING and I'm NOT (YET).

I'm going on the trip...

And if that's not bad enough, every teacher suddenly seems to want to talk about the SCHOOL ACTIVITY TRIP as well.

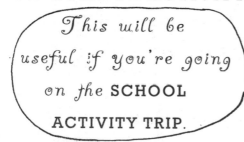

This will be useful if you're going on the SCHOOL ACTIVITY TRIP.

OUTDOOR SPORTS

Mrs Worthington even says SCHOOL ACTIVITY TRIP in MATHS!

"The **SCHOOL ACTIVITY TRIP** is for THREE DAYS. There are NINE different activities to do, so how many could you do each day?"

(The answer is NONE in my case ... as I might not be going.)

On the way home, Derek can see I'm a bit fed up. So he tries to make me laugh by telling me what happened in his class today.

"Someone - I don't know who - DREW a FUNNY picture of Mrs Nap dressed as a BEAR like she did for **Book Week**."

So I say, "Did you get into trouble, Derek?" (I guessed it was him.)

"It was close, but I managed to RUB out her FACE before Mrs Nap came in and saw it and told me to SIT down and stop drawing ALIENS on the board!"

Derek shows me a small version of what he drew.

Mrs Nap

It's genius and does cheer me up. ☺

The FIRST and most IMPORTANT thing I'm going to do when I get back is to MAKE SURE MUM or DAD fills in my SCHOOL ACTIVITY TRIP FORM.

If I forget to bring it in AGAIN, I'll have no chance of going.

(Which would be a DISASTER for me.)

When I get to my house, I notice there's a group of people standing in next door's front garden. Which is a bit ODD.

Mum thinks so too, because I can see 👀 her *peering* through a tiny gap in our living room curtains. She's still watching them, even when I wave at her.

A very **O**ld lady called Mrs O'Leary used to live in that house. When I was little, Mrs O'Leary would tell me that she was

ONE HUNDRED AND FIFTY YEARS YOUNG, you know!

I thought it was **TRUE** until Delia pointed out that NOBODY is that old and only an **IDIOT** would believe her.

"That makes you an idiot, Tom," she'd tell me, being a nice sister. 🙁

Then a few months ago Mrs O'Leary moved

out (BYE!) to live closer to her

family, leaving the house

`empty` until now....

So I'm deliberately taking my

time to open MY front door

while having a sneaky peak at

exactly who's next door.

There's a lady with a clipboard.
She's chatting to a man and a lady
with a girl (who <u>could</u> be my age,
I'm not sure?).

They're all about to go inside when
the girl turns around and catches me
STARING at her. She SNEERS at
me at first...

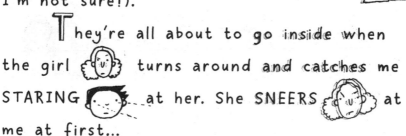

THEN she only goes and pulls

a REALLY STUPID FACE!

huh?

I wasn't expecting that.

Hmmmmmm.

    I COULD just ignore her.

        OR ...

I could do THIS ⬇ RIGHT BACK AT HER!

BLAHHHH!!

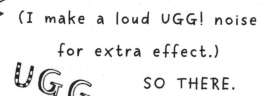

Then she pulls ANOTHER face at me and sticks out her tongue as well. I put down my bag and use BOTH hands to STRETCH down my eyes and pull ᵁᴾ ⬆ my nose.

(I make a loud UGG! noise for extra effect.)

UGG   SO THERE.

Mum's **TAPPING** on the window trying to get me to **STOP,** because **EVERYONE'S** LOOKING at me now.

Tap tap

Oh

Shame

I want to shout "SHE STARTED IT!"  but by the time I've stopped looking at Mum, the lady with the clipboard has already closed the front door and the girl's gone inside.

When I come into the house, Mum looks a bit cross.

"What were you doing pulling SILLY faces, Tom?"

The girl STARTED it!

Mum says, "That's NO excuse. You should have IGNORED her instead of joining in PULLING SUCH a

HORRIBLE FACE!"

Delia is back from college early and *SLOPES* in at EXACTLY the same time as Mum says

"HORRIBLE FACE!"

Which is not good timing because straight away she LAUGHS and says,

"I agree ... it's a HORRIBLE FACE."

"Go away, Delia - Mum wasn't talking about that."

"What - your HORRIBLE FACE?"

Mum corrects Delia by saying, "Tom was pulling a HORRIBLE face, he hasn't got a horrible FACE."

"That's a matter of **opinion**," she says.

"Ok, enough!" Mum says; then she adds,
   "Anyway, far more importantly, we've got
people looking at next door's house."

 "New neighbours?" Delia asks.
"I'm not sure yet," says Mum.
Mum is being [extra] NOSY. She suggests that
NOW might be a good time for her to
hang out some washing
in the garden.

(Which really means Mum wants to have a
snoop and listen in to what they're saying.)

But that's OK because while Mum's trying to spy on the neighbours, I can disappear up to my room with a packet of snacks. **I**t's messier than usual because I was a bit late going to school this morning. **I**'m digging around trying to find that FORM **M**r Fullerman gave me. (I'm sure it's in my bag.) I get sidetracked by TWO SWEETS that have slipped down into the lining. I can FEEL them there ... I just need to find out how to GET them ... left a bit right a bit. NEARLY ... done it. YUM, unexpected SWEETS are the best! They're almost as good as finding another layer of chocolates that no one's eaten yet.

YES!

The sweet wrappers are a bit **STICKY** so I'm trying to pick them off carefully when I notice I can see right into next door's garden. It's been empty for a while - I hadn't really looked much before. The man outside is pointing at the ROOF while the other lady is looking round the garden.

That RUDE-face girl is busy hitting flower heads with her stick.

(Mum won't like that.)

She's been outside hanging up <u>ONE</u> tea towel for **AGES** while trying to peer over the fence and listen in at the same time.

I'm still watching when Delia comes out to ask Mum a question. Knowing Delia, it's probably something like, Can I have some money?

Then Delia glances up at the window and catches me staring at her. She MOUTHS the words

HORRID FACE at me and shakes her head.

OK, Delia, I'll show YOU what a REALLY horrid face looks like. I press mine RIGHT up against the glass until my nose gets completely squashed (that way she'll be able to see all the way up it). My eyes go all WONKY and I get a flat face too. Serves her right. I get a bit carried away SQUISHING my face against the window ...

... and forget all about **M**um.

And the new neighbours, who are lòöking at me **AGAIN.**

(Groan.)

Mum stops hanging out the tea towel and comes back into the house. I have to promise **NOT** to pull any more faces.

Yes, Mum.

We're both upstairs when the doorbell goes (which gets me off the hook).

It's Granddad **B**ob, who's just popped round on his mobility scooter for a visit while Granny Mavis is shopping.

Hello

Tra -la la!

Mum offers him a cup of tea and I follow them because in our house:

TEA + Granddad = BISCUITS

Granddad Bob asks, "Who were all those people coming out of next door's house?"

Mum says, "Possibly our new neighbours – or n**o**t, if Tom's put them off."

Granddad says, "That young girl was a bit cheeky. She stuck out her tongue and started to pull SILLY faces at me for no reason at all."

And straight away I say,

 "See, Mum? That's what she did to me too." ← Girl

Then Mum says, "Yes, but I told you not to pull a SILLY face back at her, Tom, didn't I?"

Granddad says, "Hey, Tom, I bet your silly face wasn't as good as the one I pulled!" Mum is looking at Granddad and shaking her head. Granddad's face-pulling is VERY impressive.

Mum says, "Please tell me YOU didn't pull that face in front of our NEW neighbours ... did you?"

That will be a YES, then.

My granddad is a legend.

My school planner is supposed to REMIND me of **IMPORTANT** dates and events that are going on in school.

And the *KITCHEN* calendar is where FAMILY stuff like birthdays 🎂 and holidays ☼ are all written down so EVERYONE can see what's happening (and won't forget).

Groan

Most of the time, I find out what's going on like this.

TOM, GO AND GET READY FOR _ _ _ _ _ _ _ _ _ _ _

Fill in the blank here.

It could be a visit to the cousins 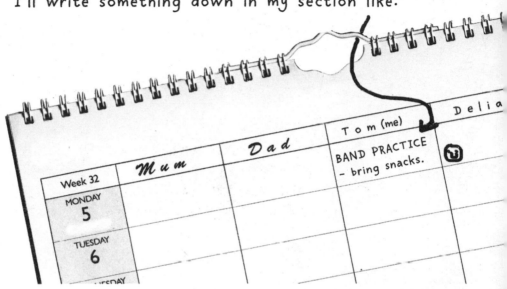 or Aunty Alice's birthday... Occasionally I'll write something down in my section like:

Week 32	M u m	D a d	T o m (me)	Delia
MONDAY 5			BAND PRACTICE – bring snacks.	
TUESDAY 6				

But Mum still ends up having to remind me about it.

Sometimes I have **FUN** writing extra stuff in other people's sections. Like this:

	M u m	D a d	T o m (me)	D e l i a	
ek 32			BAND PRACTICE – bring snacks.	☺	
NDAY 5	Shopping				
JESDAY 6	pick up Granny Mavis from YOGA				
EDNESDAY 7		Work "do" in evening			
THURSDAY 8					
FRIDAY 9					
SATURDAY 10		FITNESS PROGRAMME starts today			
SUNDAY 11		And ends HERE Ha! Ha!			

It's taken Dad a WHOLE week
to spot this one.

He tells me,

"I'll have you know, Tom, that RIGHT NOW my body is a TEMPLE."

Then he starts doing lots of really embarrassing muscle man poses.

Mum's laughing at Dad posing. She says, "More like a Temple of Doom," then brings out the shopping list and crosses off BISCUITS for Frank.

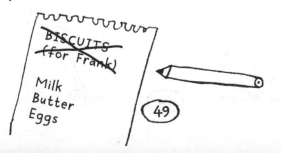

BISCUITS
(for Frank)

Milk
Butter
Eggs

"I'm assuming you don't want me to buy biscuits that might ruin your 'TEMPLE', Frank?"

Dad tells us, It takes a lot of hard work to look this good, you know.

Mum and I leave him flexing his muscles and pretending to do press-ups on the wall while we head off to the

SUPERMARKET.

100-101-102

Oh dear

Normally I would [avoid] shopping with Mum –
but for some reason,
FOOD shopping isn't quite
so bad.

In the CAR, Mum's about to drive off
when Uncle Kevin pulls up next to us.

He hops out to say hello, so Mum opens her
window.

HI, Rita!

He says, "I was just passing, so I thought I'd
check that everything's still OK?"

Mum looks puzzled. "Everything's GREAT, thanks, Kevin."

"It's very good of you to help out, Rita." From the LOOK on Mum's face, I can tell she has NO idea what Uncle Kevin's talking about. But she still says,

"Of course, it's NO problem, Kevin." Then Uncle Kevin asks ME... "Are you sure you don't mind, Tom?"

Mum's giving me the EVILS in case I say something stupid – like, "We've got NO idea what you're talking about, Uncle Kevin."

(Which wouldn't be the first time.)

So I just play along and say,

"I don't mind at all."

Luckily Uncle Kevin adds... "The boys are really looking forward to staying over with you."

And **SUDDENLY** Mum remembers what's happening. "Of course! It's ALL on the *kitchen calendar.*"

(It's not.)

Uncle Kevin looks at his watch.

"I'll go and say hello to Frank while I'm here."

"We've just left him FLEXING all his muscles," Mum tells him.

"That shouldn't take too long, then!"

Uncle Kevin is still LAUGHING at his joke when we drive off.

Mum says to me, "Your dad will be surprised to see Uncle Kevin, won't he?"

(Yes he will.)

SUPERMARKET Special

Part of going food shopping with **M**um is being able to *sneak* a few "extra snacks" into the trolley when she's not looking.

→ → → →

I don't always get to keep them, though.

I'm only buying essentials, Tom

Custard creams ARE essential

I spend most of the car journey telling **M**um how WELL I did in school this week (for a change). Fingers crossed she'll be in a REALLY good mood and happy to treat me.

I don't tell her the **WHOLE** story about how
MARCUS MELDREW tried to put me OFF
 my reading, by STARING at me with his
EYES ➡ CROSSED. (Mum doesn't need to
hear about any more
funny faces.)

BESIDES, I played a good {trick} on
Marcus later that day and pretended his
EYES ⊙̀ ⊙́ were ⊂⊃ ⊂⊃ crossed AGAIN.

"Uncross your eyes, Marcus," I told him.

"They're not crossed," he said.
"They REALLY are ... and if you don't
UN-CROSS them, they might stay like that
FOREVER."

"How come I can only SEE ONE of you if they're CROSSED, then?" he asked me.

So I told him, "THAT'S a VERY BAD sign. It means your eyes are starting to STICK like that already."

(I was very convincing.)

Marcus wanted to see for himself, so he asked to go to the toilet. When he came back, he said, "My eyes are FINE. I'm not falling for THAT trick again."

I pointed out thet he must have WOBBLED them back into place when he stood up. Ha! Ha!

(Mum didn't need to hear any of that stuff.)

So here I am at the **SUPERMARKET** with Mum and her LIST (which she likes to try and STICK to).

Mum says, "Thank goodness Uncle Kevin reminded me about your cousins coming to stay.

I have NO idea WHEN they're coming, though. Not too soon, I hope."
(Me too.)

"I'll look on the *kitchen calendar* - it MUST be written down." It's definitely NOT, and I know why.

Huh?

— Hello, Kevin. Of course they can come and STAY. I'm writing it in the calendar now.

We grab a trolley and head to the  **FRUIT**

and **VEGETABLE** section.

There's a  *Special Offer*

on a **BIG SUPER SAVER** BAG OF **BANANAS.**

 Mum puts one in the trolley and says,

"Bit green, but they'll ripen up."

Normally I would wait
for a good covering
of shopping on the
bottom of the trolley

before attempting to sneak in a treat.

But I don't have the
chance because Mum
has brought out ANOTHER ...

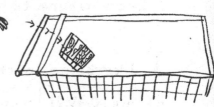

"I nearly forgot, I've got this mini list for you to do if that's OK, Tom?"

OWN LIST ✚ OWN 🛒 TROLLEY

= OWN TREATS → Treats

Yes, Mum, I can do that.

"I'll be here so come straight back, no messing around, OK?"

It's not a BIG SUPERMARKET — I know where to go so this won't take long.

I like being in charge of my own trolley.

On the **list** I have to get...

o Cereal  – that's easy. ✓

o Chocolate spread 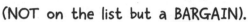 ✓

(NOT on the list but a BARGAIN).

o Fizzy sherbet ✓

(not on the list – but

for the cousins).

o Onion rings ✓

(not on the list – for

me and the cousins).

o BAG of SELF-RAISING FLOUR – whatever. ✓

o BAG of CASTER SUGAR – tick. ✓

(Shopping is a *breeze*.)

o SUPERSIZE PACKET OF TOILET ROLLS

(largest pack).

I'm looking up and down the aisle

and I had **NO** IDEA there were SO many ...

... different types!

Quilted, extra soft, recycled, extra thick, budget, packs of two – six – twelve – different colours. I read the list again – SUPERSIZE, it says. But they all look the same size to me?

I'm confused.

Until I spot the **BIGGEST** pack I've ever seen.

(Yep, that's them.) ⟹

I try and lift a pack down from the shelf. It's not heavy, just tricky to hold. I'm struggling to carry it and I can't quite see ☉ ☉ where I'm going or where I left my trolley?

It's here somewhere – here we go.

I SQUASH the MASSIVE pack of loo roll
down into the trolley
and head back
to where Mum is.

On the way I make a quick detour to
grab a pack of caramel wafers
and wedge them down the back.
THERE - all done. ☺

I can hear someone calling

Tom! It must be Mum so I do a super-spin
turn in the trolley and BUMP right into...

AMY PORTER?

"What are you doing here, Amy?" I say.

AMY says, "Same as you, Tom ... or I WAS until you PINCHED my trolley."

"HUH! DID I?"

"YES, you did, I saw you. Our shopping's under that **MASSIVE** pack of toilet rolls."

"Oh yes ... so it is."

(That's embarrassing.)

"**W**e need to **swap** trolleys, then – follow me."

(I feel like I'm doing the **SUPERMARKET** walk of SHAME.)

AMY says, "That's a LOT of toilet rolls."

(Oh great – as if this wasn't AWKWARD enough, I have to chat about TOILET ROLLS too.)

So I just say, "They were on my list." And wave my list at her.

LIST

AMY's mum is chatting with my mum, who's standing next to my trolley, which is **FULL** of stuff that's NOT on the list.

AMY's mum says,

"It's easily done, don't worry, Tom!"

"I wondered why you were taking a while," Mum says. (She's spotted all the extra goodies I have.)

I say, "It's all for the cousins... OK, some stuff's for me."

AMY says, "You've squished our tomatoes and bread, Tom."

(Whoops – so I have.)

AMY's mum says, "We'll get more."

Luckily the toilet rolls haven't squished my caramel wafers.

I grab the wafers and shove them into our trolley behind the toilet rolls again. Only somehow I manage to accidentally *rip* the plastic that's holding the rolls together. Two of them fall out

and BOUNCE on the ----ground.

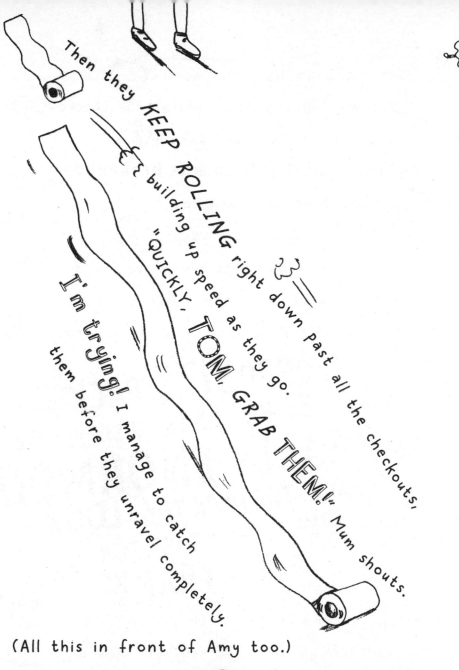

Then they KEEP ROLLING right down past all the checkouts, building up speed as they go.

"QUICKLY, TOM, GRAB THEM!" Mum shouts.

I'm trying! I manage to catch them before they unravel completely.

(All this in front of Amy too.)

I just want to go home now.

But we STILL have to pay at the checkout.

The man on the till asks Mum,

"This toilet-roll pack is broken; do you want a new one?"

And Mum says,

"Thank you, that would be good."

The man announces to the WHOLE

SUPERMARKET through a loudspeaker:

"SUPERSIZE PACK OF TOILET ROLLS to till SIX PLEASE. THE REALLY ENORMOUS PACK. THE PACK THAT LOOK LIKE IT WILL LAST FOR ... ABOUT A YEAR?"

That's not true - but he thinks it's funny.

(I've had enough of toilet rolls for one day.)

We're loading up the car with the shopping when we bump - into **AMY** and her mum **AGAIN**. Mum is busy trying to **FIT** all the toilet rolls into the boot (which won't close). So she starts passing me individual toilet rolls to put on the back seat. (It's like playing a game of toilet-roll pass the parcel.)

AMY says, "Those toilet rolls are a lot of trouble, aren't they?"

I say, "YES - they are."

Then I suddenly remember something that's NOT a lot of trouble. My *caramel wafers!* I take them out of the bag and offer **AMY** one. "**G**ood job I remembered to take these out of your trolley!" I tell her. **AMY** says, "Thanks, Tom. Did you remember to give in your **SCHOOL ACTIVITY TRIP** form as well?"

"NO!"

I t's been nearly a WHOLE week since

M r Fullerman gave me another form to fill

in (which must still be in my room somewhere).

A s we drive home,  Mum tells me

not to worry. She says, "There's nothing

you can do about it now, Tom. I'll fill it in

when we get back."

That's the plan.

Back at home, I go and search for my Form straight away. I think it's buried in my MESSY room ... well, I hope it is? At last! It's under a pile of

ROCK WEEKLYS. I take it downstairs and Mum fills it all in while Dad unpacks all the shopping.

No biscuits?

Mum makes a suggestion...
"So you don't miss the trip,
why don't I pop into school with the form and
have a quick WORD with someone?"
"What sort of word do you want to have?" I
ask Mum (thinking the worst).
"Don't worry, Tom, I'll ask Mr Fullerman or
Mrs Mumble about the trip very nicely. We
don't want you to miss out."
Then (as usual) Delia manages to turn up and
join in the conversation.

She adds,
"And MUCH more importantly, we want to get rid of you for a few days."
"That's not true," Mum says.

"OK ... for a few weeks, then."

(I ignore her.)

Dad wants to know why we've bought SO many bananas?

Mum says, "We're going to have lots of visitors, so don't worry, they'll all get eaten."

Then Delia says unless we've got a family of chimps coming for tea we might struggle to eat THAT many bananas - which annoys Mum a bit.

BIG Super Saver BANANAS

"They were on {special} offer—
I'm trying not to spend too much."

Delia says, "Speaking of money,
can I borrow some for the bus fare?"

 **M**um and **D**ad forget about the
bananas and tell **D**elia that:

1. She can't keep asking them for
   money all the time.

   Can I have some money

2. She's old enough to get a Saturday job.

I'm standing behind Mum and
Dad nodding my head in agreement,
which would normally drive Delia ...

 BANANAS.

Ha!
Ha!

But today she just says...

"Please can I have some money — or I'll be **LATE**."

And Mum says, "**LATE** for WHAT? You didn't tell us you were going out. It's not written on the *calendar*."

Now I'm wagging my finger at her.

Delia says, "I'll be late for **work**."

WORK? Mum and Dad look shocked.

"Yes, work. I've got a job. I'll give you the money back when I get paid," she tells them.

Mum wants to know where she's working (and so do I).

"At a food place, in town – only for a few hours. But it's a job, so be happy, OK?"

Dad hands over some money with his mouth open. Delia *rushes off* and leaves them both looking a bit **surprised.**

I take the opportunity to sneak in (what I think is) a very good suggestion.

"Now you don't have to worry about Delia, does that mean there's more pocket money for me?"

I'll take that as a NO, then.
(Worth a try, though.)

 **M**um says I have to tidy my
room JUST IN CASE the cousins
turn up to stay.  hello

I agree to tidy a bit.

As I'm SQU**EE**Zing a few things under my bed
(which does the tidy trick for now),

I see Derek in his room from my window.

He holds up a card with a very good idea
on it.

Game of
MONSTER
BATTLESHIPS?

I hold up a
sign that says ...

 It's a useful game in situations when you're a bit bored but need to keep QUIET.

Once in a particularly LONG and boring assembly, we played it sitting at the back of the hall.

It's like normal battleships only with MONSTERS instead.

Here's how we play it:

 There's a KING monster – worth 20 points.

And a QUEEN monster – worth another 20 points.

 Then there are five mini monsters – worth 5 points each.

And five BLOB monsters, each worth 1 point.

You draw a square and number them like this...

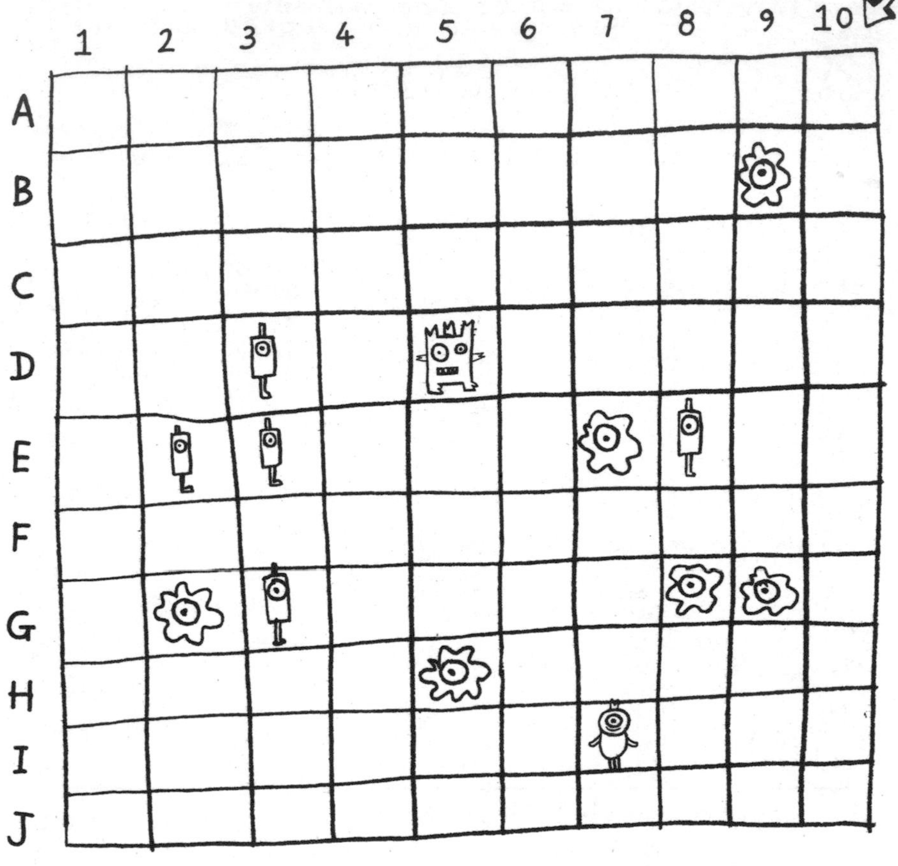

Then you draw all your monsters in different squares.

B9 · E7 · G2 · G8 · G9   D5

D3 · E2 · E3 · E8 · G3   I7

$\mathbb{D}$erek writes down what square he's going for and holds it up to the window.

He's already **HIT** one of my monsters! AGGGH!

Then it's my turn.

(I missed.)

He's got another one of my monsters!

$\mathbb{W}$e keep playing until Derek's mum comes in and says he has to go to bed. Derek won this time.

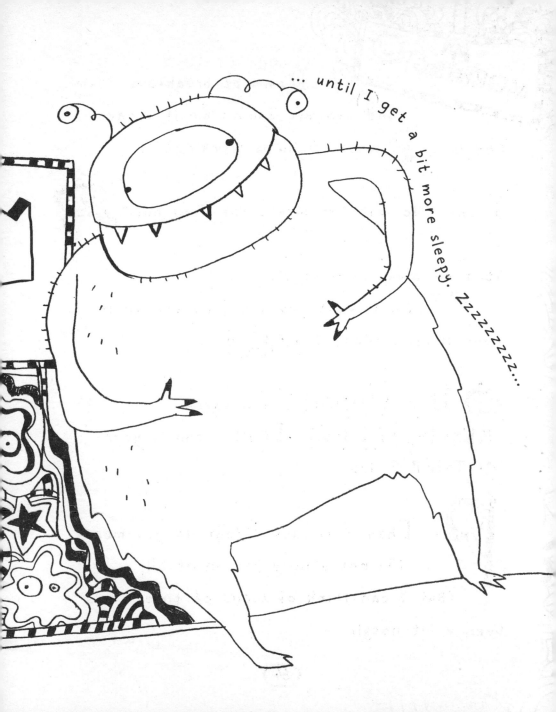

MORNING!

Down at breakfast, Mum and Dad are asking me if I have any idea where Delia is working?

I say, "No, but I'm sure I can find out!"

Straight away Mum says,
"I don't want you snooping around in your sister's room, Tom."

Dad LAUGHS and says,
"Absolutely not, Tom - that's your MOTHER'S job."

Then Mum says, "What do you mean? I'm not a nosy person at all!"
(But I can think of loads of times she's been a bit nosy!)

So I say, "What about when you were pretending to hang out washing so you could hear what the NEW next-door neighbours were talking about?"

Mum says, "I had lots of wet washing to hang out. I wasn't pretending!"

So I remind her that she only had ONE tea towel. Which makes Dad LAUGH.

"When did we get new neighbours?" he asks. I tell him how they were looking around the house next door and how the little girl was REALLY annoying. "For no reason at all, she KEPT on pulling faces at me ... like this..." (I demonstrate.)

Delia comes down for breakfast and says, "That's a BIG improvement, Tom, you should stay like that."

(Very funny, Delia.)

Dad says, "Morning Miss I've Got a Job."

Which makes Delia say, Oh pleeease.

Mum asks her where she's working again.

Delia says, "What does it matter? If I tell you, I know what will happen. The WHOLE family will turn up to BUG me."

(THAT'S a good idea. I REALLY want to find out now.)

Delia says grumpily, "I'm going now - and I'll be late home tonight because I'm WORKING."

86

Mum starts shoving bananas at her as she leaves.

Groan

"Take one for a snack
... take two."

I've just noticed my cereal is covered with chopped bananas as well. Which is not how I'd normally have cereal, but I don't mind – I like bananas.

Just as well, really. We've got LOADS.

87

My **SCHOOL ACTIVITY TRIP** form is on the fridge with a LARGE STICKY note that says DON'T FORGET (so I won't forget).

Don't forget

I manage to persuade Mum NOT to come into school for a word after all.

There's no way I'll forget my form now, because Mum's stuck reminder notes EVERYWHERE I look.

Derek POPS by to see if I'm ready to go to school yet. *You ready yet?* (Not quite; nearly.) While I'm upstairs brushing my teeth, Dad's chatting to Derek downstairs.

"Are you going on the school trip, Derek?"

"I hope so."

Then I hear Mum asking Derek if he can:

1. Make sure I give in my form?

2. Take a banana with him?

"We've got plenty."

It's like Mum doesn't trust me! Which is annoying. I RUN downstairs and grab my bag for school. Then Derek and I both say *BYE!* before rushing out of the door. We're only halfway down the road when the look on my face tells Derek that ... NOOOOOOOO!

Mum's waiting for me at the door
with the form in her hand.
(Along with another banana
in case I get hungry.) Got it!

At school, ➡ Mr Fullerman says I can
take my form to the office.
So straight away I go off to see
Mrs Mumble, who's on the phone.
While I'm waiting for her to finish her call,
a family comes in and stands behind me. Mrs
Mumble puts her hand over the phone and says,
"I'm sorry, I'll be
with you in a minute.
Please take a seat."
Not to me – to the family
behind me, who all go and sit
down. I turn round to have a look.

There's a GIRL who looks very familiar?
As I'm staring at her ... she starts doing stupid bunny teeth at me.

NOW I REMEMBER! ➡️

What's SHE doing here in my school?

Mrs Mumble comes off the phone.

"What's this, Tom?" I give her the form but I get a bit distracted by the GIRL and BLURT OUT...

It's my ACTIVITY 🐰 RABBIT FORM, Mrs Mumble.

Which makes no sense at all.

"Do you mean your SCHOOL ACTIVITY TRIP form, Tom?"

"YES."

"It's a bit late. But we've had a few cancellations so you might be lucky."

I tell Mrs Mumble that I'm sorry it's late but I really want to go and if she can do anything to make sure that I'm on the list that would be ABSOLUTELY AMAZING.

She says, "You might be in luck. We've had a couple of cancellations already."

Which is EXCELLENT NEWS.

Then Mrs Mumble says to the waiting family, "Welcome to Oakfield School! Mr Keen will be with you very soon."

I hope that girl's not coming to MY school! And if she is, fingers crossed she's not in my class.

That **would** be BAD NEWS – unless she sat next to Marcus and annoyed him instead. (Which **might** work?)

With my form SAFELY given in, I go back to class to catch up with one of my favourite subjects.

ART

(Things are looking up!)

Mrs Worthington is teaching our lesson today. "Put down paper all over the desks so they don't get too messy."

Mrs Worthington wants us to get a brush, a water pot and choose one colour of paint to do our pictures. (Less paint to clean up, I suppose?)

Norman Watson is already in trouble for *FLICKING* paint on to his paper.

Most of it's gone on Pansy's back.

Stop flicking paint, Norman!

Next Mrs Worthington says, "Find a lovely object to paint using the techniques I've just shown you. If you want to take anything from the table over there to paint, please do." (Mmmmm, not really.)

"Or you might have something of your own instead?"

That's an idea. Shame I didn't bring any caramel wafers with me today.

I'm rummaging through my bag and I find a couple of Granny's cocktail sticks left over from the cheese and banana hedgehog she brought round. And I find ANOTHER  banana...

Granny's banana hedgehog

I Poke the sticks into the banana so it
looks a bit like an alien.
AMY brings a small
plant back to the table and for SOME
reason Marcus has chosen a woolly
SOCK with individual toes to paint.

Mrs Worthington is walking around,
giving tips on what to do next. *"Good start
on your sock, Marcus."*
Marcus suddenly moves his arm and JOGS me.

I SPLODGE paint all over my paper just when Mrs Worthington comes to look at it.

"*Mmmm, interesting combination, Tom.*"

I try and tell her what happened. "It was a mistake... Marcus jogge..."

But Mrs Worthington's already gone to stop Norman from FLicking more paint.

I say, "Thanks a lot, Marcus, for jogging me."

He says, "I didn't touch you! It's not my fault your picture looks like a ...

SPLODGE."

Mmmmm, this splodge reminds me of someone.

"Can you guess who this is, Amy?" I ask her.

She guesses straight away.

Ha! Ha! Ha! Ha!

While I'm waiting for my picture to DRY,

I take the —————→ cocktail sticks out of

the ⟨banana⟩ and ⟨think⟩ ❀ about eating it?

That's when I notice that the banana

skin has turned **BLACK** where the cocktail

sticks went in.

I gently poke one of the sticks into the

skin again – and it starts to turn **black**

αlmost straight away. OK – this could

be good.

So I do a few more dots and start to build

up a doodle.

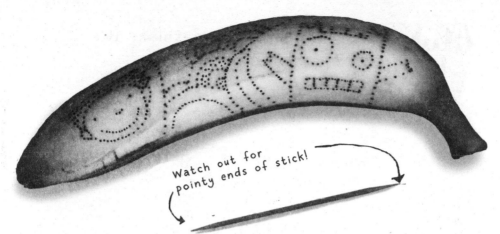

Watch out for pointy ends of stick!

AMY wonders what I'm doing, so I show her.

"That's **AMAZING**," she says.

It's good, isn't it?

I do another banana doodle in the fresh side.

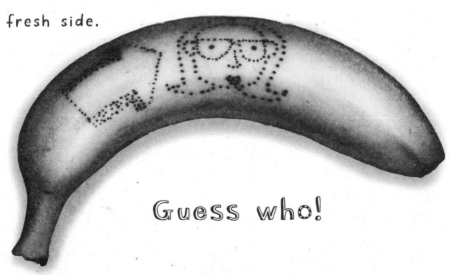

Guess who!

AMY is very impressed and thinks it's **FUNNY**. And Marcus, who's being nosy, is looking at it too.

"What's that?"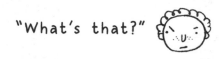

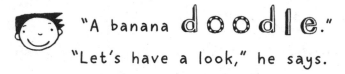 "A banana doodle."
"Let's have a look," he says.

Marcus wants to know how I did it. So I say, "It's easy, I'll show you."

Dot dot dot dot dot dot dot dot ... dot.

"There you go ... that's how you do it."

Marcus is studying the banana closely. As the dots get darker, he says, "OK, I get it now ...

is THAT MRS WORTHINGTON?

So I say, "Keep your voice down, Marcus. I don't want Mrs Worthington to see it."

See what, Tom?

(Too late.)

Mrs Worthington says, "That's very creative, Tom. You've done a DOT drawing on a banana..." (I have.) "And that looks a bit like me?"

Uh-oh, I'm in trouble now...

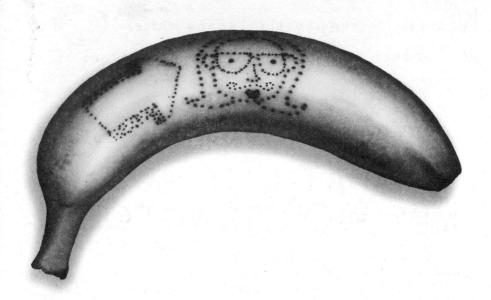

"Stay behind after class, Tom."

(I'm guessing Mrs Worthington has just seen the extra moustache dots.)

Groan.

(Could have been worse, I suppose.)

EVEN MORE bananas **News...** has travelled *FAST* about my **banana tattoos** and how to do them. Bananas have never been so popular in school. They're everywhere!

I've been doing a few e x t r a banana doodles at home too. (You can still eat the banana as long as you don't leave them for TOO long.)
This one is for Delia.
I told her it was a
        present. Ha! Ha!

The pile of bananas Mum bought was gradually going down when Granny Mavis came round with a WHOLE lot more.

"Hello! I know how much you all like bananas and they were SUCH good value."

(Luckily she didn't bring another one of her banana hedgehogs.)

But she had made some banana and pepper biscuits.

Norman and Derek turned up for band practice just in time to eat some.

We're supposed to be writing new songs for **DOGZOMBIES**. But it's so easy to get distracted. Granny gives us a plate of biscuits to take up to my room with us. Norman eats most of them.

I get out my guitar and TRY to think of things we could write songs about. Norman suggests How about bananas?

Maybe (maybe not).

"Or about a dog called Rooster?" Derek says because we can all hear him BARKING in the garden.

Norman wonders if our favourite band in the WHOLE world – **DUDE 3** – would write about a pet dog?

So far the songwriting is **NOT** going very well.

We have a few more ideas from

looking at stuff around my room.

Pillow song

Blanket song

I see through the **WINDOW**

Window song

Then I suggest we could look at the pile of

ROCK WEEKLYS  for inspiration?

"**D**elia's got more in her room, I'll get them,"

I tell them. They agree.

It's a **GREAT IDEA**.

Delia's Room Ha! Ha!

I think Delia's at work (wherever work is), so she won't catch me snooping around.

While I'm in there, I spot something that looks VERY ODD and out of place in Delia's room.

It's a little white HAT. I've NEVER seen her wear anything like that before?

I grab the ROCK WEEKLYS and put the hat on my head.

Norman and Derek think it looks stupid on me.

It looks stupid on them too.

As we're looking through the **ROCK WEEKLYS** this PAGE GETS MY ATTENTION.

CALLING ALL DUDE3 FANS!

Here's your chance to design a T-shirt for **DUDE3**.
DUDE3 are looking to their fans to come up with an original design for a T-SHIRT that will be printed and WORN by the band themselves.

Send your designs to the address below

With your name:

Address:

And contact details:

Competition deadline is

Songwriting is abandoned (for now). Instead I get out all my ✏️ pens, paint and paper and we all have a go at doing some T-shirt designs.
Norman's paint FLICKing works out a bit better this time.

Derek's drawing is pretty good too.
My doodle T-shirt design takes a while - worth it, though.
Dad pops his head round the door to see how the songwriting is going.
(It's not.)

DUDE3 ROCKS

DUDE3 Yo!

Then he says,

I've got a special tasty snack for you all too. Three guesses what it is?

Hello!

Not more bananas, I say. Groan.

Bananas ... with a difference.

Dad's gone and stuck a wafer on each of them. Thanks, Dad! →

(It's a very good idea.)

He likes our T-shirts too.

Norman tries to eat his while Derek and I go straight for the wafers. We save the bananas for later (after I've done another quick doodle on them). We're just finishing off our T-shirt designs when Delia comes STORMING into my room. She SHOUTS,

Where's my HAT?

So I say...  "What hat?"

"The **ONE** you took from my room, along with those **ROCK WEEKLYS** too," she says, looking at all her magazines. I try to keep a straight face and tell her, "No hats around here." (Derek and Norman are keeping OUT of this.)

"**I need** it for **WORK** - so you better give it back **FAST**." Then Delia suddenly spots her hat ... the banana's wearing it.

Delia snatches the hat back and shouts, "**K**eep **OUT** of my room!"

I wait until Delia's left before making Derek and Norman LAUGH like this.

Ha! Ha!

SCHOOL NEWS!

In class,

Mr Fullerman says he has

an announcement to make.

Looking at the expression on his

face, I can't tell if it's going to be

GOOD news, BAD news or both?

So we're all waiting ... and waiting...

"It's about the school trip," he says.

(He's really stringing this out...)

"If you've put your name down on the list,
I can tell you now that you..."

(YES, what!)

"You'll ..."

WHAT!

"... ALL be going on the trip."

PHEW! That is GOOD news.

It's not long before we go either, so that's just as well. Then he tells us (and here comes the BAD news bit), **"Everyone will be expected to take notes on all the interesting experiences you'll be having on the trip."**

Really?

"Each of you will be given a VERY special journal to write in."

(And hopefully draw in too?)

Mr Fullerman shows us some of the journals that other kids have done in the past.

(They're a bit good.)

"As you can see, it's a GREAT way of remembering your trip."

Mmmm, I guess so. Sounds like a lot of work to me. The journals are a bit nicer than our usual schoolbooks — which is good... And there's no other homework to do while we're writing our journals. EXCELLENT!

Mr Fullerman hands out more LETTERS about the trip too.

There's a LIST of STUFF we have to bring. The only thing I don't have is a waterproof coat, but Derek has two so I can borrow one of his.

At break time I double-check that's OK with Derek. No problem PHEW!

I say, "That means I won't have to go clothes shopping with Mum." Which is always a relief.

Derek asks me if Delia is still MAD at me? And I say, "She is, but that HAT has made me want to know where she works even MORE."

This is cute, Tom

Not for me

(I'll have to find out when I get back from my trip – Mum and Dad really want to know too.)

I've **also** noticed that now I'm definitely going on the **TRIP** – not one teacher has mentioned it in any of my lessons! (When before, they wouldn't stop going on about it!)

Which is **annoying**, because I'm so excited I can't stop thinking about the trip ...

in class ...

and at home.

But Mum and Dad are driving me a bit **BONKERS** about the trip.

You'll need lots of extra-warm VESTS

Sigh

You can take this woolly hat with you, Tom

Oh great

I'm only going for THREE DAYS  but from the way Mum's fussing about things I have to pack, you'd think it was THREE WEEKS!

Box of plasters

All your PANTS

And toothpaste

Extra socks

Delia's been out a LOT and I haven't seen that HAT  again since the banana was wearing it.

As I'm off tomorrow on the trip,

THE FOSSILS have come round to say BYE.

Granny Mavis says,

"I've made you a little 'something'."

(Which is nice of her.)

It doesn't look like a little present to me?

It's not.

Granny's knitted me a HUGE jumper with a MASSIVE smiling banana on the front!

"You'll grow into it, Tom. It'll keep you warm on your trip," she tells me.

"Thanks, Granny," I say. I don't mention it might not fit in my bag. Granddad gives me some banana biscuits "for travel snacks".

He bites into one and pretends it's broken his teeth.

Which makes Granny sigh. I

crack

give them both a HUG and go off to pack the rest of my stuff.

I discover that (SOMEHOW) Mum has managed to sneakily pack my bag already.

So I just need to concentrate on the **really important** stuff instead (my snacks).

Some of the other things Mum wanted me to take — I leave out.

 Shower cap?

Eye mask?

(I keep the plasters. They might be handy.)

Tonight I'm going to bed EARLY. I don't want to be late (as usual).

I'm **very** EXCITED.

Mustn't forget to bring my ACTIVITY trip journal either.

Plasters are useful already. ↗

AWAKE!

The Journey

Just for a CHANGE I managed to wake up NICE and EARLY so I could:

1. Get into the bathroom **B.D.** (which stands for **B**EFORE **D**ELIA).

2. **D**ouble-check I hadn't forgotten anything important for my trip (like my swimming trunks – because THAT'S happened before).

3. **M**ake a VERY BIG decision – teddy or no teddy?

(I decided to bring teddy – but hide him.) Then I SQUEEZED my case shut and headed downstairs for breakfast. ☺

I was in a really GOOD mood until I bumped into Delia coming out of her room. She *pushed* past me and said,

> Haven't you gone yet?

Which I thought was a stupid question to ask. So I told her, "If I'd GONE, I wouldn't be here, would I?"

Then she said, "Well hurry up and go, will you?" - before accidentally *TRIPPING* over some tins of paint and brushes that Dad had left at the bottom of the stairs.

Dad was in the kitchen and called OUT:

> MIND the tins of paint and the brushes at the bottom of the stairs

just a little bit **too** late.

> Enjoy your *trip*?

I asked Delia. Which I thought was FUNNY even if she didn't. Ha!

 I left my bag at the front door, then headed to the kitchen, where I could

smell something DELICIOUS being cooked.

I t was (PANCAKES!) MY FAVOURITE. :)

Mum said pancakes would keep me going "all day, on your REALLY **long** journey."

(Thanks, Mum!) :)

Delia (who was even MORE grumpy now) said, "What **long** journey? He's only sitting on a coach for two hours, **not** trekking up a MOUNTAIN."

(True – but I'm happy to have pancakes any time. Mmmmmmmmmmm.)

Trekking up a mountain is exactly the sort of thing Tom might be doing on his trip,

Dad said.

Which was a worry, because I don't remember seeing anything about TREKKING UP MOUNTAINS on the list of activities?

* Climbing
* Trekking up mountains

(127)

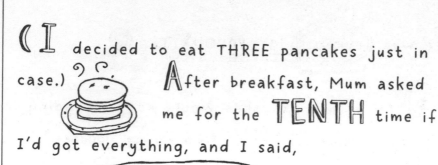

(I decided to eat THREE pancakes just in case.) After breakfast, Mum asked me for the TENTH time if I'd got everything, and I said,

 YES, I've got EVERYTHING.

Even your toothbrush?

 Apart from my toothbrush.

(I didn't mention I'd forgotten to brush my teeth as well.)

For the ELEVENTH time Mum asked me,

 Have you got EVERYTHING?

And I said, YES ... I think so.

Then Dad carried my bag to the car while I said BYE to Delia.

128

"**A**re you **STILL** here?" she asked.

 "**I**'m leaving now." Finally,

Delia said grumpily.

Then she stood by the front door to watch us go.

When I got in the car, Mum told me, "We'll miss you, Tom. Even Delia will miss you!"

But from the way Delia was PUNCHING the air and pretending to celebrate as we drove off, I'm **not** so sure. ➡ ─Yes

When we got to school, everyone was already sitting on the coach waiting for me.

> **Hurry up, Tom, you're a bit late,**

Mr Fullerman told me as we arrived.

Being late wasn't such a **BAD** thing because **M**um and **D**ad had to say goodbye to me quickly without too much fussing or hugging. (Phew.)

All the kids in my class were watching,

including Marcus Meldrew. Who for <u>some</u> <u>reason</u> was **STARING** at me with his **EYES CROSSED** (again).

Derek managed to save me a seat behind Solid and Norman, who was so excited he could hardly keep still.

When the coach finally set off, all our mums, dads, friends, families and even pets waved goodbye.

All the kids CHEERED and waved back. (Apart from Julia Morton, who was already feeling coach-sick.)

The SCHOOL ACTIVITY TRIP had begun!

HOORAY!

Straight away, Derek and I got out our snacks to see what we both had to eat.
It was an excellent selection.

Derek said, "This FEAST will last us for AGES."

YUM

CRISPS

Soft Jelly sweet

Before

After

(It didn't.)

Most of the girls, including **AMY PORTER,** were sitting together at the back of the coach and

SINGING REALLY LOUDLY.

Normally, **M**r Fullerman would get **CROSS** and say, **That's enough singing, girls** **OR** **Too loud!**

But as this was supposed to be a **"FUN TRIP"** he let them keep singing ♫ (for a while, anyway).

Derek suggested we could play that **YES or NO** game. Which was a good idea, as Derek had come prepared with **sticky notes** and everything.

He wrote something down quickly and stuck it to my forehead.

133

 Solid was already LAUGHING at what it said. "That's a good one," he told me. Which made it MUCH harder for me to think of something good that Derek could be. I thought I'd picked something FUNNY – but Derek guessed it SO

QUICKLY!

nlike me. I took ages to guess what I was...

Am I alive?   Yes.

Am I a singer?   No.

Have I got legs?   Yes.

Am I famous?   No.

Am I Rooster?   No.

Am I an animal?   Kind of.

    (This went on and on and on...)

    Eventually I said,

        Derek just said,

I'd never have got that. A flea was a good creature to choose.

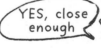

After our game, it was SNACK TIME.

I rummaged through my bag to take out my snack box (again). But I kept finding little **notes** that Mum must have *slipped* into my bag.

Miss you, Tom xx

Brush your teeth Mum xx

Mum!

"My mum likes to write me notes," I told Derek. "Did she write this one as well?" Derek asked.

Tom, you have rotten teeth

ha! ha!

"I think Delia did that one."

(Typical.)

As I'd eaten most of my snacks already, the only things I had left were the banana biscuits Granny Mavis made and the slightly green bananas.

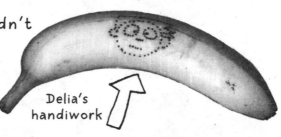

Norman said he'd eat one if I didn't want them. "Help yourself" I told him before I realized that DELIA had been doodling. (She'd got the banana doodle idea from me. Though Norman didn't seem to mind eating it.)

Delia's handiwork

This seemed like a good time to have a go at drawing something in my journal. It wasn't easy drawing on a moving coach.

Cheese puff

My monster doodles looked a bit wobbly...

The coach journey went really = FAST and before we knew it Mr Fullerman was announcing,

> **We're here. Make sure you don't leave anything behind on the coach.**

Everyone got more chatty and lively as we turned in to the Activity Centre (apart from Marcus, who was asleep and dribbling).

Mark Clump was about to wake Marcus up when Norman did it for him.

BOo!

As we got off the coach, the Activity Centre Team Leaders cheerfully said "HELLO" and showed us the way to the hall.

We took our bags and waited to find out who we'd be sharing the CABINS with.

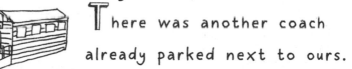There was another coach already parked next to ours.

But none of us took much notice of it, as we were all too busy looking around.

I told Derek,

The FUN starts HERE!

(Or maybe NOT?)

The team leaders handed out TIDY CABIN FORMS.

(Which didn't look like much fun to me.)

Activity Centre
TIDY CABIN FORM

Summer Cabin B

	TIDY	CHECKED	POINTS
DAY 1			
DAY 2			
DAY 3			
DAY 4			

BIG PRIZES FOR THE MOST POINTS!

I'm good at some things - but being tidy isn't one of them.

We were given MAPS of the centre too. I've stuck mine here so I don't have to keep explaining where everything is, which is handy.

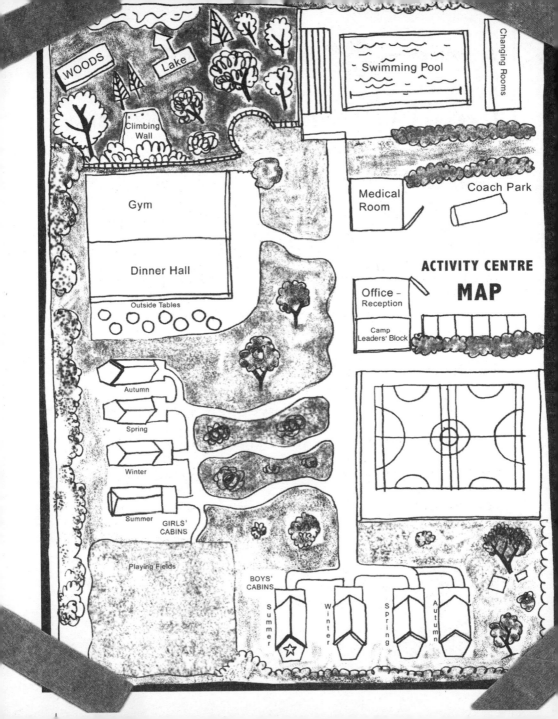

I marked my cabin with a STAR on the map.

I was in SUMMER CABIN B, along with: Brad, Norman, Solid, Marcus (I can't get away from him!), Leroy and Mark.

Derek was in a different camp with his class – SPRING CABIN B – it was next door to ours, so not that far away.

You can see on the map there were two more cabins nearby called (you guessed it) AUTUMN and WINTER.

All the cabins had wooden floors and nice comfy bunk beds (brilliant!). Inside the wardrobes there were separate sections for each person sharing a bunk bed, along with a mirror and a few more drawers to stuff things in. Our bags were kept on a rack by the door.

 But the only person who could
reach the top was Solid
(which was handy).

I was going to share with

Solid, who really wanted to sleep on the TOP
BUNK.

But he got stuck climbing up and changed his mind.

It's too
tricky for me,

he told me. Brad
Galloway and Norman
had already started to

run round the room, jumping
from bunk to bunk.

Mr Fullerman
stomped into the cabin and
pointed to his room with a WARNING.

I don't expect to be disturbed by you lot larking around all the time, so you'd better BEHAVE, BOYS!

They replied, "Yes, sir."

(But not in a very convincing way.)

Unpacking didn't take me long at all. It's AMAZING what you can stuff into a wardrobe with one hand.

Solid reminded me that we were supposed to get changed into our sports kit for this afternoon. Which meant taking everything OUT again.

And that's when I found these:

Love U Tom xx

MORE of Mum's NOTES (groan).

She'd put this one in my trainer.

MISS YOU!

146

I couldn't find my sweatshirt - but I knew it was in there somewhere.

I got distracted when Norman (who was still a bit hyper from all the snacks on the coach) decided to *ROLLLLLLL* in a straight line under all the beds while saying...

HELLOoo

It was quite funny right up until he rolled on to Mr Fullerman's feet.

Get off my feet, Norman, and up off the floor too.

Mr Fullerman had already told everyone, **"You're only at the Activity Centre for THREE DAYS, so it REALLY doesn't matter what bed you choose."** (It did to Marcus.)

He had a MASSIVE sulk about what bed he was in.

"I won't be able to sleep ZZZZZ if I don't have the end bed," he told Mark Clump

(who had the end bed).

Mark Clump said, "OK, I'll swap because I can get a MUCH better a view of the BATS from this bed."

Marcus looked shocked.

What BATS?

"The BATS in the woods over there," Mark said. "They like old trees and sometimes they sleep in barns ... OR maybe even cabins like this one."

Leroy Lewis asked if the BATS would BITE.

Big-foot

I'm
nice

"They're not VAMPIRE bats!" Mark assured us.

All this talk about BATS was making Marcus a bit TWITCHY.

"What do you mean,

VAMPIRE BATS?"

"NO - not vampire bats - normal bats. They hang out in corners of rooms or gaps in the ceiling."

Mark Clump told Marcus there was no need to be scared of bats. And Marcus said,

"I'm not scared of BATS - I'm not scared of anything."

(If you say so, Marcus.)

roan

Then Marcus only went and asked Mr Fullerman if he could move beds AGAIN! He said, "I can't sleep in the corners – I really need to be in middle bed on the TOP bunk."

(I was in the middle bed on the top bunk.)

Mr Fullerman sighed and told him,

"You don't want to be late for lunch. If Tom doesn't mind moving, that's OK with me."

I was very hungry and just wanted to EAT – so I said, "FINE, I'll move." And I told Marcus I'd get all my stuff later.

Before we left for lunch, I managed to just quickly grab my sweatshirt from the floor and followed Mr Fullerman out of the cabin.

On the way to the dinner hall, **M**r Fullerman

told us who we were sharing the centre with ...

GREAT MANOR SCHOOL.

Which made us all groan. That school is SUPER

good at everything.

(**O**akfield School vs Great Manor School

≅ a **WIN** for Great Manor School every time.)

Their kids had **already:**

Neat
clothes

Arrived early and changed.

Done an activity.

Eaten lunch.

Not like us Oakfield School kids – we only

just made it to lunch.

My
unpacking

I was standing in the lunch queue choosing
what to eat (pasta or chicken – both?)

Ha!
Ha!
Ha!

when I could hear
LAUGHING coming from behind me.

Ha!
Ha!

Derek was already eating – so I chose
the pasta and went to sit down
with him. More people started
laughing, which made me wonder
what was so FUNNY?

Derek and I compared lunches first.
(The same.)
Then cabins. "Any BATS in yours?" I said.
"None that I know of," Derek said.

AMY PORTER and Florence Mitchell

walked past me and THEY
started LAUGHING too.

When Marcus joined in I'd had ENOUGH
and asked him,

Ha! Ha!   "What's so funny, Marcus?"

He said,
"YOU ARE, TOM!"

Then Derek spotted something STUCK on
my back and took it off.

"This might be the reason people
are laughing."

It was only ANOTHER one of MUM'S NOTES.

To MY lovely
TOM - MISS
YOU **LOADS**

KISS KISS
from Mum XX

Yuk

Groan.

(Fingers crossed there are NO
more of Mum's notes anywhere!)

 FIRST ACTIVITY *YEAH!*

 After lunch, Team Leader JOE came to collect us. He wanted to know...

Are you READY to get started?

And we all shouted, "**YES!**"

Then he asked,

"**Hands up if you like building and making things?**"

I [LOVE] making stuff, so I got carried away and shouted,

"**YES, ME! I do!**"

a bit too loudly.

"**Calm down, Tom,**" Mr Fullerman said.

(It's Norman who usually gets overexcited.)

When Derek was put in the same group as me, I got **EVEN** more excited. (Along with Solid, Norman, Indrani, Marcus and Julia – who said she was feeling much better now.)

I think Derek and I are pretty good at making things (if I do say so myself).

Last week we made an **EXCELLENT** den in the garden. It was a **VERY** good place to hang out when:

1. Mum wanted me to tidy my room.

2. Delia was looking for her latest copy of **ROCK WEEKLY**.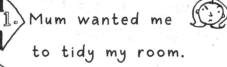

3. Dad kept asking where his biscuits had gone?

Yeah!

Spider builds stuff

Ant sand-castle

keep OUT

Biscuits

Joe and the other team leaders showed us some STUFF laid out on the grass.

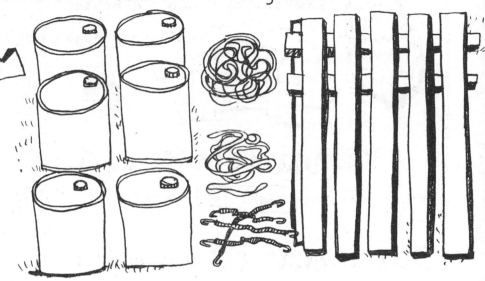

"Can anyone guess what you'll be making today?"

Brad Galloway thought it was funny to whisper, Cupcakes? He got a BIG

GLARE from MR Fullerman.

(I laughed.) Mark Clump suggested we could make a SPACESHIP!

(I could see that sort of working.)

Someone else said, "A house?"

(Maybe, maybe not.)

Then **AMY PORTER** said,  RAFTS?

Which was the | right ✓ | answer.

Joe told **AMY** "Well done," and

explained what he wanted us to do.

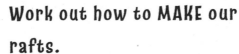 1. Think about how to DESIGN our rafts.

2. Work out how to MAKE our rafts.

3. Use the materials provided to BUILD our rafts.

Joe said it was "very important to work together as a team."

(Which was easier said than done with MARCUS in our group.) Groan

He kept suggesting **WEIRD** ways of putting the raft together.

It took us quite a while – but finally, with Team Leader Jenny's help, the raft got (sort of) finished.

← Snail race

Mr Fullerman and the team leaders congratulated us all on

finishing your first activity!

Team Leader Joe said, "We'll see whose RAFT is going to be the winner in the raft race tomorrow!"

RAFT RACE – WHAT RAFT RACE?

"I'd forgotten about that," Solid said.

He wasn't the only one.

Building a raft is one thing – RACING it was something else.

"I hope the race is a short one," Derek said.

"I'm not sure our raft will make it."

He had a point.

FIRST night in the CABIN

Norman, Leroy and Solid wanted to have a midnight FEAST.

Which was a brilliant idea.
But I'd eaten most of my treats on the journey (apart from two tattooed bananas).

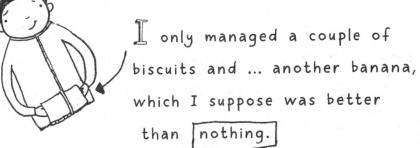

So at dinnertime I tried to SNEAK out some extra food under my sweatshirt.

I only managed a couple of biscuits and ... another banana, which I suppose was better than nothing.

On the way to our cabin, we got chatting to some kids from Great Manor School who seemed nice enough.

T hey told us about the climbing **wall** and how
HIGH it was. **M**arcus Meldrew said,
"That wall doesn't look high to me!"
Even Solid (who's really **TALL**)
thought it looked a bit scary. Marcus boasted,
"I've climbed higher."

"When was that, Marcus?"
Derek asked.

"On holiday – it was a
massive mountain. That wall will be easy
for me to climb," Marcus insisted.

We'll see, I said. Then I reminded
Marcus that all my stuff was
still in his wardrobe.

I really need it back, I said.

Nice biscuits

Marcus just took everything out and dumped it on my bed.

Which would have been OK — if only another one of Mum's notes hadn't fallen out of a sock!

I managed to **grab** it before Marcus read it out **loud** to everyone.

PHEW!

(Mum had only gone and mentioned my teddy in the note — which would have been EXTRA embarrassing.)

Brad Galloway suggested that as WELL as a midnight ☾ feast, we should play a few TRICKS on some of the other kids.

What kinds of TRICKS?

Mark Clump wondered.

Hiding stuff in people's beds, that kind of thing.

"What, like an apple crumble bed?" Norman said.

I told him, "It's an apple pie bed."

"YEAH! We should do one of those."

The only problem was, none of us knew how to do an apple pie bed.

164

Mr Fullerman came into the cabin and thought we were all just making our beds neatly.

He said, **"Well done, lads"** and gave us our first POINT on the TIDY CABIN sheet.

Activity Centre
TIDY CABIN FORM
Summer Cabin B

	TIDY	CHECKED	POINTS
DAY 1			
DAY 2			
DAY 3			
DAY 4			

BIG PRIZES FOR THE MOST POINTS!

Mark Clump had <u>another</u> idea.

"Hey, I've got another idea!"

Then he went outside to find a pine cone.

"What do these remind you of?" he asked us.

"It's a pine cone, stupid," Marcus said.

"A mini Christmas tree?" Which was true - they do look like tiny trees - but it wasn't what Mark wanted to hear.

"**N**o - they look like ...

... MICE."  (Really?)

Mark said, "I'll show you. Just tie a piece of string around the end of the cone, then you pull them along the ground."

STRING

Leroy still had some string from making the rafts - he gave it to Mark so he could show us.

"There, what did I tell you?"

(The pine cone still didn't look much like a mouse.) We squinted - and that seemed to help.

Then Mark put the pine cone under his bedcovers and gently pulled the string towards him.

OK - we all got it now.

Norman and Solid made a Sock snake too.

It was perfect timing when a group of kids from Great Manor School walked past our cabin.

Brad SHOUTED, "HEY, LOOK, there's a mouse or some kind of weird CREATURE in our cabin! Come quickly!"

They came to the door and looked around. "Where's this creature, then?" one kid asked. And we all pointed to the bed, where the mouse shape was beginning to move.

Mark Clump
was hiding by
the bed, holding the
string, and began to pull it
towards him.

"What's *THAT?*" one kid said.
"I'm not sure, but it lööks ... suspicious,"
another one said.

(We were all trying not to LAUGH.) Then
one of the little kids said, "I know what we
should do with that kind of creature."

He slowly took off one of his shoes and gave the lump an almighty ...

WHACK!

Then another

WHACK!

Until it stopped moving ...

completely.

(169)

Gul

"There, all sorted," he said. "You won't be bothered by that creature any more."

We all looked SHOCKED.  But then the Great Manor kids burst out LAUGHING as they left the cabin.

Ha! Ha! Ha!

I'm guessing they knew it wasn't a mouse all along. (They did.)

"We're the ones who've been tricked, I think," Solid said.

(We had.)

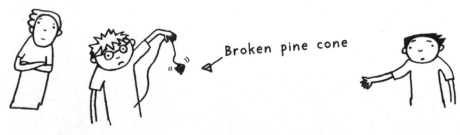

Broken pine cone

Midnight feasts and tricks

While the team leaders were busy telling everyone to **get ready for bed,** I was busy searching for my pyjamas. Which seemed to be missing.

Luckily Solid came to my rescue with an **EXTRA-LARGE** spare T-shirt which came down to my knees. At least I had something to wear now, even if it did look a bit like a nightdress.

Thanks, Solid

Phew.

Our first night in the cabin started out with Mr Fullerman reminding us,

"We've got a **PACKED** day tomorrow, so you'll all need a good night's sleep."

(Norman didn't look sleepy at all.)

Mr Fullerman said,

"Lights out – sleep tight and don't let the bugs bite!"

"What bugs, sir?"
Norman wanted to know.

Mr Fullerman assured us all that it was just a saying. **"There are no bugs really."** Then he closed the door and turned off the lights.

Mark Clump waited until Mr Fullerman had gone before he told us,
That's not true, there are LOADS of bugs around.
Norman asked,
In the cabin?
Mark said,
Yes, spiders and that kind of thing are everywhere.
No one wanted to hear that before going to sleep. Mr Fullerman popped his head around the door again to remind us,
Oh, and NO midnight feasts or loud snoring either, please!
We all said, "Yes, sir." Two minutes later, we all started chatting again.
Norman whispered,
Is it midnight yet?
Which made us laugh.
Ha! Ha! Ha! Ha!

Solid tried to get out of bed quietly but EVERY floorboard he he stepped on CREAKED LIKE CRAZY

when he put his foot down.

Sorry, he whispered. I suggested it would be easier for Solid to stay in his bunk.

We'll come over to you and Marcus.

That way Solid wouldn't wake Mr Fullerman up. So one by one, we crept over quietly and sneaked out our SNACKS for the midnight feast. ✳ ☾

(Which wasn't at midnight ...
✳ ✳

... or much of a **feast** either.)

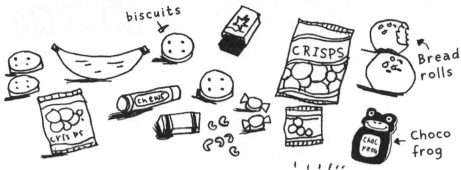

biscuits

CRISPS

Bread rolls

Choco frog

Granny Mavis would have been proud of [my] snacks, though. I had four biscuits and a banana, so I made biscuit banana sandwiches and gave one to Solid. (They were a bit squishy but tasted OK.) **N**orman had a packet of crisps.

He ate them while shining a torch underneath his chin to make scary faces. Marcus Meldrew said he couldn't share his sweets because he'd only got four sweets left. But I could hear him in the dark, secretly unwrapping and eating A **LOT** more than four sweets.

Sneaky sweets

Then Brad Galloway suddenly remembered that he still had a LARGE packet of **POPCORN**.

He said, (We can share it,) which was nice of him.

Norman shone his torch on the ground so Brad could get the popcorn.

CREAK

Mr Fullerman was still moving around in his room. Leroy said, "SHHHHHHHHHhhhhhh" while Brad stood like a statue in case he came back in.

Still

Freeze

Brad waited until it was safe to move. Which took a while. He crept back and tried really hard to open the popcorn. "I can't do it!" he whispered.

Grrrr

POPCORN

So Solid tried next.  Grrrrrrr.

(It wasn't happening.)

Then Norman and Leroy did their best to open the popcorn. Which didn't work either, so I I had a go.

 It still wouldn't open.

Marcus GRABBED the whole packet from me.

"Give it here, you lot are useless. I'll open the popcorn."

Marcus only went and SAT on the

POPCORN. OOOOFFFFF.

It WENT BANG! and EXPLODED EVERYWHERE!

178

Mr Fullerman came running in and turned on the lights.

"WHAT IS GOING ON?" he said.

(It didn't take long to find out.)

We had to clean up as much popcorn as we could before going back to bed and promising - no more feasts, snacks, or messing around.

"Is that CLEAR, boys?"

"Yes, sir."

After he'd closed the door, we kept quiet for a tiny bit longer than last time.

Right up until Mark Clump said he could hear a BAT.  "Where?" I whispered.

"Outside, flying around," Mark said.

"Not a vampire BAT?" Leroy wanted to know. We all got up and lOOked out of the window. I couldn't see any bats.  But we could hear Mr Fullerman heading towards the door again. Everyone JUMPED back into bed as fast as possible.

Then Brad Galloway whispered...

"There's a SNAKE in my bed!"

"Ssssshhhhhhhhh,"

we told him.

"It's only our sock snake," Norman said.

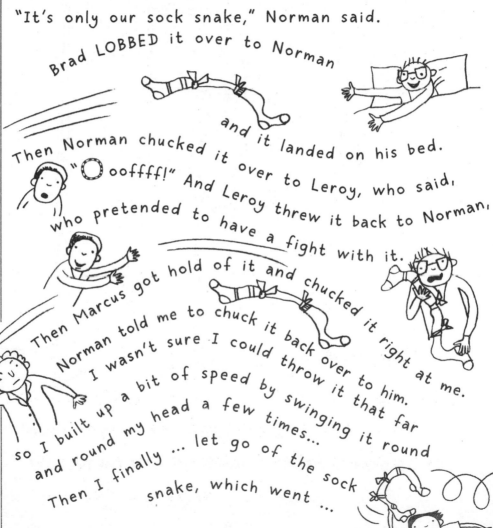

Brad LOBBED it over to Norman

and it landed on his bed.

Then Norman chucked it over to Leroy, who said,

"Oooffff!" And Leroy threw it back to Norman,

who pretended to have a fight with it.

Then Marcus got hold of it and chucked it right at me.

Norman told me to chuck it back over to him.

I wasn't sure I could throw it that far

so I built up a bit of speed by swinging it round

and round my head a few times...

Then I finally ... let go of the sock

snake, which went ...

socks

ZOOMING through the air and landed right on

MR Fullerman's HEAD just as he turned the lights on.

"THIS is your LAST chance unless you want to be doing written work all day tomorrow."

Sorry, sir. (We didn't.)

 Morning!

Lovely day!

Sun plaster

I thought Mr Fullerman would be in a REALLY BAD mood this morning, after our (sort of) midnight feast and sock snake episode. But he was surprisingly JOLLY and very WIDE AWAKE. Not like me.

This was because when everyone else eventually dozed off, I discovered that BRAD GALLOWAY talked in his sleep. He had a WHOLE conversation with his eyes closed about dogs and how he wanted to take them for a walk.

I tried to wake him up - but nothing worked. He just said,

Wake up, Brad

There's a good boy, ready for your WALKIES.

He kept talking all night and didn't remember a thing in the morning.

(183)

I hoped Brad wasn't going to do that every night or I might have to swap beds again.

Thanks to Brad's "CHATTING" I was a bit sleepy at breakfast.

Team Leader Jenny shouting, "Morning, everyone!" woke me up a bit. "I hope you all slept well and are ready to have some FUN!"

(Kind of.)

She told us our rafts had been moved to the lake and were ready for the RACE. (GREAT.) "So let's go!"

Team Leader Joe led the way.

We followed them through the woods to the lake, where anyone taking part in the race had to put on a helmet and a lifejacket. Marcus insisted on being at the back of the raft.

Sleeping monster

"I can steer it and be in charge," he said.

"Whatever, Marcus," I said (like we had a choice).

Team Leader Joe reminded everyone, "Paddle carefully, as ⟶ straight as you can, to the finish line. Can everyone do that?"

We all said, YES (even if we couldn't).

Looking at our raft - I wasn't sure it would make it that far. Great Manor School were taking part in the race too and their rafts looked a bit different to ours.

Team leader

Julia suggested we should all paddle at the same time (it was a good plan).
But Marcus was too busy **FLicking** water at Norman and wasn't listening.
Then Norman flicked water back, only most of it went on to Mrs Worthington, who was trying to take photos for the school newsletter.

She shouted, "*Stop that, you two!*"

When Team Leader Joe BLEW his whistle for the race to start, we all began to paddle like **cRAZY** – but not at the same time – or in the same direction. Our raft wasn't going very far, mostly just round and round in circles. "PADDLE TOGETHER," Julia told us (again) as we went round for the **THIRD TIME.**

Marcus stood up (which was a mistake).

"Sit down, Marcus," Derek said because he was making the raft WOBBLE.

Eventually we started to move forward very slowly and WAY behind the other rafts.

I could hear CHEERING at the side of the lake from the other kids, which kept us going. Paddling was HARD work.

Just as we got closer to the team leader holding the finish-line flag, Marcus managed to DRAG up a LARGE bit of lake weed with his paddle, which landed on NORMAN'S legs. He tried to shake it off, which made the raft start ROCKING sideways, backwards and forwards. "STOP moving, it's making me feel sick!" Julia shouted. Then Marcus STOOD up, which made Norman lose his balance and topple into the water...

(187)

followed by me, Derek and lastly Julia.

Marcus pretended he didn't know HOW that had happened. We all managed to splash him as we fell in, so he wasn't completely dry. Great Manor School won the race (which was no surprise). And our team came last, but that didn't matter because being in the lake was actually fun (it wasn't very deep).

Our team got out and went back to the cabins to change out of our wet clothes and get ready for an afternoon of wall climbing. Which I hoped would be as much fun as raft racing turned out to be.

Yeah!

As Marcus Meldrew was the only one not to fall in the water — it was even more annoying having to listen him going **ON** and **ON** about how "wall climbing is EASY because I'm VERY brave, you know."

(Really, Marcus...) So it was a bit of a surprise when at the **FIRST SIGHT** of the WALL, Marcus suddenly developed a VERY bad case of stomach ache.
Which got worse and worse the more he stared UPWARDS at the WALL.

Norman said he couldn't WAIT to start climbing and wanted to go first.

It was AMAZING how *f a s t* he managed to **WHIZZ** up to the top.
"Go Norman! Go Norman!" we shouted – which made Marcus groan and hold his stomach even more. Mr Fullerman decided that Marcus should miss out the wall climbing and go to the sick bay instead.

(And that seemed to cheer him up.) 😊 When it was my turn, I was a bit slow, but got there in the end (just). Coming back down to the ground turned out to be an adventure too.

Groan

BUMP!

Everyone, except Marcus, managed to climb the very high /WALL\ .

I would have had a LOT more sympathy for Marcus if I hadn't caught him SCOFFING LOADS MORE SWEETS when we got back to the cabin. *huh?*

He said the sweets had made him feel better AND ... he could definitely climb that wall now. (No problem) (Knowing full well it was too late.)

Solid told Marcus, "Climbing the wall was a LOT harder than it looked." After hiding his sweets, Marcus said, "It didn't look that hard to me."

"How would YOU know?" I wondered. And Marcus said, "It wasn't my fault I got a stomach ache, I'm a $good$ climber and BRAVE too."

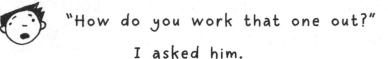

"**Y**ou're **not THAT** brave," I said, which was **true.**

"Well, you're not either," Marcus said.

"How do you work that one out?" I asked him.

"**A BRAVE** person wouldn't need to bring a cuddly-wuddly teddy bear to bed with them."

HUH?

Marcus had been snooping.

"Thanks a lot, Marcus," I said, feeling a bit embarrassed.

Then Brad said, "What's wrong with having a teddy bear?" Turns out I wasn't the only person hiding a soft toy after all.

"I can't sleep without mine," Leroy said.

Which **SHUT** Marcus up.

Though if I was **N**orman, I might have kept quiet about having a

SNUGGLE BLANKET.

"Doesn't anyone else have a snuggle blanket, then?"

No, just you, Norman.

(It looked a bit manky too.)

DINNER TIME

Here's a picture of my `` `empty' '' plate because I **SCOFFED** [all] my dinner tonight as it was the BEST! AND I had seconds of ice cream too.

Tiny chip crumbs left

Marcus couldn't finish his after all the secret sweets he ate earlier. ~ Yuk

Team Leader **J**enny told us we had a little something else to look forward to now as well.

Then she handed everyone a small package or envelope to open.

(194)

I got two letters and some caramel wafers. Even though we're not away for THAT long, it was nice to get a letter and TREATS!

(I'm guessing the teachers brought everything with them – so we all got our letters at the same time.) Here's mine:

Hello, Tom!

We hope you're having a GREAT time doing lots of EXCITING activities at the centre.

The house is very quiet without you. But while you've been away we'll be busy painting your bedroom (it will look great when you get home!) and making it MUCH tidier too. Which won't be difficult.

Here are a few wafers for the journey home. Don't eat them now.

We'll see you very soon.

Much love,

Mum and Dad xx

Then I got a **SURPRISE**, as the other letter was from ... Delia.

Tom,

I wish I could say I was missing you but that would be a lie.

While you're away Dad's going to paint and decorate your bedroom. He couldn't decide what colour to do it. So I suggested a mixture of stripes and spots might be nice ... in different colours.

When you get back, you might need a pair of my sunglasses to look at it.

Granny Mavis is making you a WELCOME HOME CAKE. I hope you like cabbage.

I told her it was your favourite so it will be in the cake.

(Ha Ha) From Delia x

Then I noticed there was a P.S. on another page.

P.S. I found your DUDE3 design-a-T-shirt competition entry. You forgot to POST it, numbskull.

P.P.S. It wasn't bad either.

NO WAY!

$\mathbb{I}$'d worked SO hard on that design too. I can't believe I forgot to post it.

$\mathbb{M}$arcus offered me a sweet, I looked so fed up.

"No, thanks," I said.

(I hardly EVER say no to sweets.)

Want a sweet?

Groan

Owl Trouble

Summer Cabin B (that's us) had been RUBBISH at getting points on the TIDY ROOM chart. We all kept forgetting to make our beds and that kind of thing. Derek told me that his cabin (Spring B) were trying to be EXTRA neat because apparently there's a MASSIVE PRIZE for the tidiest cabin at the end of the trip. There is?

He says that Mrs Nap's in charge of the prize "so who knows what it will be."

First prize

Abacus

Talking about PRIZES, I showed Derek the letter from Delia – he read the first part and said,

 "**I**'m so glad I don't have a sister."

"It gets worse, read the last page," I told him. **D**erek shook his head. "**Oh no!** How did you forget to post your T-shirt competition design?"

 "Who knows, I just forgot," I said.

T-shirt design hidden

MESS

(I think this might have been why.)

Derek was gutted for me. He thought I might have won too. "You never know, there might be another competition you can enter," Derek said, trying to be all cheerful for me.

 "Yeah, maybe."

(I'm pretending to be OK – but inside I'm doing this...)

 AGH!

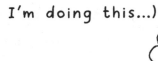

Getting back to the (very messy) cabin – Solid thought it would be funny to hide in the wardrobe (which was a bit of a squeeze), then ═══ *LEAP* out at whoever opened the door.

Which in this case ... was ME.

SURPRISE!

I got a bit of a

~SHOCK,~

but at least it took my mind off NOT posting my T-shirt competition design for a bit. **N**orman said he wanted to be a bat and sleep up^side do^wn tonight.

He told everyone, "It's quite comfy."

(It didn't look comfy to me.)

Norman changed his mind when his face went all **RED**.

I told him, "Your face is as red as Mr Keen's when he's angry."

When **M**r Fullerman came in to tell us about tonight's campfire treat, he did a quick head count to check we were all in the cabin.

Where's Solid?

We pointed to the wardrobe, where he was hiding again. **M**r Fullerman opened the door and SOLID *LEAPT* out at him, SHOUTING,

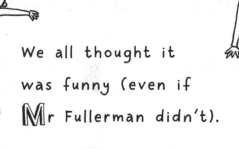

BOO!

We all thought it was funny (even if **M**r Fullerman didn't).

11

I'm writing this by torchlight because
BRAD is TALKING in his SLEEP AGAIN!
Which is beginning to freak me out a bit.

He's mumbling something about MARSHMALLOWS...

I think he's reliving the campfire treats we
had tonight.

      That's what it sounds like.
    It was a FUN evening, which
started out nicely enough.

Mmmm,
yummy hot
chocolate.

zzzzzzz

Here's what happened...

Our team leaders organized a wonderful campfire for us to sit round. AND they gave us hot chocolate and toasted marshmallows too.

The teachers were all very pleased with the way the trip was going.

Phew

Relief. Nearly done They said everything seemed to be working out well. No accidents (touch wood, Mr Fullerman), no one was too homesick or sick (Marcus's stomach ache didn't count).

We were all having a great time (with just one more day to go).

Mrs Worthington told everyone not to get too close to the campfire. "You don't want anything to **SINGE** from the heat."

"Like a moustache," I whispered to Derek and made him cough on his marshmallow.

We were all chatting and enjoying ourselves when Mark Clump suddenly pointed to the sky and said, "LOOK at the BATS FLYING over there." Some kids didn't like the idea of bats flapping around. Team Leader Joe said we were lucky to see them and told us some very interesting facts.

Only he called them BAT FAX

and spoke in a loud TV sort of voice.

BAT FAX ONE: BATS aren't actually blind; they can 👁 👁 see perfectly well. So the saying "Blind as a bat" is rubbish, really.

BAT FAX TWO: a single bat can eat over six hundred bugs in an hour – which is a bit like a person eating <u>twenty</u> pizzas a day! 🍕

BAT FAX THREE: a baby bat is called a **PUP**. ←(I'm a pup)

(That's a good one – I'll tell my dad that one.)

Then Team Leader Alan cleared his throat and asked us if we'd like to hear a special campfire song?　　(Why not?)

"You can all join in." Alan brought out his guitar and was about to start singing.

When he opened his mouth, this noise came
out...

TWERRRWITTT
TERRWHOOOO

 (Which wasn't what we expected.)

Julia Morton shouted,

"WHAT WAS THAT?"

AMY said it sounded like an owl.

TWERRRWITTT
TEERRWHOOOO

There it was again.

Joe said "That sounds very much like a tawny owl in the trees. Who wants to take a look?
Everyone did.

Mr Fullerman got the MOST excited.

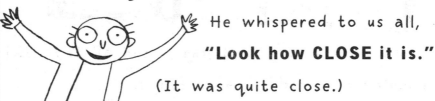

He whispered to us all,

"Look how CLOSE it is."

(It was quite close.)

We crept up as quitely as we could. Joe pointed to the owl that was sitting in the tree looking at us. Mr Fullerman said,

"That's AMAZING. Look at its feathers and those eyes. I don't think I've ever seen such big eyes on an owl before, have you?"

I whispered to Derek, "Are you thinking what I'm thinking?"

Yes he was.

Teacher   Owl

It had been a very long day – and all that owl watching had made it even longer.

Back in the cabin, I was STILL listening to Brad SLEEP TALKING

(groan)

when I finally thought of a good way to wake him up without getting out of my bunk.

hat
chat
chat

I would do my impression of an OWL hooting.

ITTERRWITT
TERRWOOO!
ITTTERRRWITTT
TERRRRWOOOO!

It was SUCH a good OWL hoot that everyone else in the cabin woke 👀 up ... apart from Brad.

ITTERRWITT   TERRWOOO!

Mr Fullerman woke up too and thought the owl was BACK. I pretended the noise came from OUTSIDE. "It's that OWL again ... it woke ME up too!" I told everyone. Mr Fullerman said he would go outside and SHOO the owl away. He told us, **"Now go back to sleep, all of you."**

Yes, sir.

I'm back!

orman and Solid's sock snake started being thrown round the cabin again.

Only this time when it came to me – I found A MUCH BETTER use for it that managed to wake 👁️👁️ Brad up.

And I got some sleep ...

Wake up Brad

eventually.

In the morning the last person to wake up was Marcus.  Looking at him *snoozing* with his mouth open, I had what I thought was an excellent idea.

I got my teddy 🐻 and the other cuddly toys from Brad and Leroy. We made them all cosy right next to him...

Marcus stayed like that right up until Norman added his SNUGGLE BLANKET. (I think the WHIFF of it woke him up.) I took a good photo to stick in my journal, though...

Today was our **LAST** day of doing activities. (Derek  said it was kayaking – which is sort of like canoeing?)

We'd all be going home in the afternoon and I was (a tiny bit) sad. ☹

WHOOP!

Yeah!

You're off!

Mind you, the team leaders didn't Seem that upset. From the way they were being all **EXTRA KEEN** and **JOLLY,** you'd almost think they were pleased to see us leave.

Before we were allowed to kayak on the lake, the team leaders brought us to the swimming pool and showed us some (important safety stuff,) along with reassuring some kids that "there are no sharks or **MONSTERS** in the lake". The Great Manor kids were already **there** ⟶

(212)

and making everything look easy
(it wasn't).

Once we got in the kayaks, Marcus said I kept getting in his way.

But he was the one wobbling all over the place. It took me a while to learn how to roll my kayak round and paddle in a straight line. Team Leader Jenny eventually told me, "Well done, Tom, that was ABSOLUTELY FANTASTIC. You're ready to kayak on the lake." Which was good news ... and right in front of Marcus too - he looked pleased for me.

The lake was A LOT murkier than I remembered it, with ducks, birds and leaves all floating around.

Marcus had to wait his turn and wasn't happy. 😠 I paddled to the other side of the lake and right back to the shallow end. Marcus was shou**ting** at me to 😠 **HURRY UP!** So I decided to go round one more time.

I carefully turned the kayak round and was about to set off again when it got STUCK.

The more I paddled, the less I moved (which was annoying). It was only when Team Leader Joe told Marcus to **"STOP HOLDING TOM'S KAYAK!"** that I realized what he was doing!

STUCK

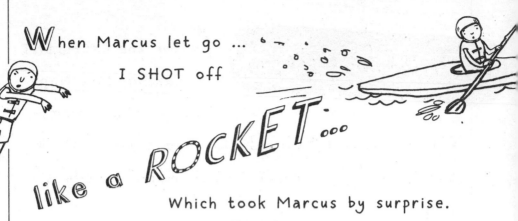

When Marcus let go ...
I SHOT off

like a ROCKET...

Which took Marcus by surprise.
He lost his balance – and landed in the lake
right next to the ducks – who looked even

more SHOCKED than

he was.

huh

At least Mrs Worthington was there to take
a few ACTION pictures for the school
newsletter.

There were going to
be some good ones
to choose from.

After the EXCELLENT kayaking, Mrs Nap told us that some Great Manor School kids had come first in the Tidy Cabin AWARD (which wasn't really a surprise).

The REAL SHOCK was finding out they'd won a MASSIVE bar of

"If I'd known that was the prize, I would have at least tried not to be so messy," I told Solid as we walked back to the cabin to get ready to leave.

I managed to pack my bag the same way I unpacked it (which didn't take long). It was a bit heavier on the way home, with a few more soggy towels and T-shirts.

STUFF

Norman suggested we should all sit at the back of the coach this time.

"It's more fun." 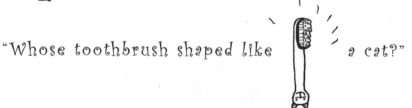 So we got a move on and tried to BAG the back seats.

Mrs Nap and the team leaders had gone round all the cabins to do one LAST check before we left.

On the coach the whole group did a

"Three cheers for the TEAM LEADERS and the TEACHERS!

Hip hip hooray!"

Then Mrs Nap held up some of the stuff she'd found.

"Whose toothbrush shaped like a cat?"

I t's Julia's.  "MINE"

"Someone's FLUFFY bed socks?"

ME

Norman said they were his.

Then she held up a smelly-looking T-shirt and a nasty sweatshirt. (No one claimed them.)

"And last but not least – who's this lovely teddy belong to, then?"

Some kids went "Arrrrrhhhhh!"

Derek nudged me and said,

"That's yours, Tom?" (Oh no ... so it was.)

I mumbled and slowly put up my arm. "It's mine."

"Who said that?"

"Me, Mrs Nap..."

"Is that TOM? Is this YOUR TEDDY BEAR, TOM?"

 "Yes ... groan."

I didn't think it was possible to make me feel any more embarrassed about my teddy.

Then she did this...

Mrs Nap made MY teddy wave at everyone as she walked all the way down the coach,

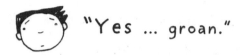
WAVE

RIGHT to the very back where I was sitting.

 Thanks, Mrs Nap

(Maybe sitting at the back of the coach wasn't such a good idea after all.)
At least I got to use him as a pillow for the rest of the journey.

Journey home

On the way back, someone spotted Great Manor School's coach, which had stopped at the side of the road. We waved as we went past and noticed that some of the kids didn't look too well.

Mr Fullerman said, **"Oh dear – looks like they ate too much of that prize-winning chocolate bar."**

Tidy cabin ✛ chocolate ✛ coach = yuck.

I told Derek it wouldn't have made ME sick if we'd won it.

As we got closer to home, everybody was starting to get a little bit excited.

I wasn't sure who was coming to pick me up. Either Mum or Dad or maybe both?

But definitely NOT Delia.

GO AWAY

220

The coach had to drive past the school first, then turn around to pull up on the right side of the pavement.

It gave us all a good chance to see who was waiting for us. Derek spotted Rooster first, then his dad. I couldn't see anyone yet.

When we got off the coach, Rooster was pleased to see Derek,

I could tell.

I told Mr Fingle that I didn't need a lift, as my mum and dad were coming to pick me up.

Derek said, "BAND PRACTICE this Sunday?" as he left. Which was a good idea.

(I'll write that on the *calendar*
when I get home.)

There was no sign of Mum or Dad
at all. One by one all the kids,
friends, parents and families disappeared and I
was the only one left.

Mr Fullerman said, **"I'll give your
mum and dad a call. Bring your bag and
come into school to wait. I'm sure there's a
good reason why they're late."** (I hope so.)

Mrs Mumble was in the school office
and so was Mr Keen. Mr Keen asked if
I'd had a good time?

"Yes, sir, I did have a great time, right
up until now."

Mr Fullerman reappeared and said that
someone was coming to collect me **"right away.
They'll be here in five minutes. They thought
you were due back tomorrow."** (Great.)

I'm home

I had to sit in the STAFFroom (awkwardly ... holding my teddy) waiting to be picked up.

I kept looking out of the window for our car to pull up with Mum and Dad in it.

SO it was a BIG SURPRISE when I suddenly caught sight of ...

Going FULL *SPEED* towards the school on their mobility scooter.

(It wasn't that fast – just speedy for them.)

They waved at me from the school grounds.

I told Mr Fullerman, "My grandparents are here." So he took me downstairs to meet up with them.

Mum and Dad were shopping,

Well?

Looks great

Sigh

Granddad told me.

"Your mum said that SOMEONE wrote in the wrong day on the *calendar*. We all thought you were due home tomorrow," Granny Mavis said.

It was nice of THE FOSSILS to come and pick me up. But they really didn't need to bring the flags.  (I'm glad they were late and no one else was here to see them now.)

Welcome home, Tom

New hat

It took me a bit longer to get home walking next to the mobility scooter.

Granny Mavis reminded me that Dad had been painting and decorating my room while I was away. I'd FORGOTTEN about that!

"It looks different," Granddad added, which was a bit of a worry.
"Different" is something I'd say when I couldn't think of anything else.

So when I got home, I went straight to my room to see what "different" really meant.

Apart from the bit DELIA had messed

with ...

My room looked AMAZING and so much tidier too. It was freshly painted white and on one wall, Dad had painted my very OWN special BLACKBOARD doodle wall.

How good was that?

Chalks

Mum and Dad weren't back yet, so I got rid of Delia's "Welcome home" message and decided to draw up a few of my favourite moments from my trip to show them when they got home.

There were lots to choose from.

GO AWAY TOM

Ha! Ha!

It was a great trip, but it's nice to be home!

Ha

Ha

THE END

I still have some plasters left – which are very good for sticking on the back of my journal.

Three days can feel like a long time to be AWAY (even though I know it's not).

It's great to get back to doing some of the things that I haven't been able to do for a while, like:

* Playing with Rooster.

* Having the bathroom to myself. (Delia's not been around much, which is also good.)

* Being back in my own bed, sleeping peacefully without being woken up by BATS or chatting. (I don't miss that at all.)

A few other things happened when I was away.

Mum managed to find out exactly WHEN the cousins were coming to stay after all.

And it's THIS weekend.
(She had to take a sneaky peak at Aunty Alice's calendar to find out.)

Ah ha!

I write everything in

AND THIS sign went up next door,

SOLD

which has sent Mum into EXTRA NOSY mode. She's desperate to find out who's moving in. She says, "I hope we find out soon."

(I just HOPE it's not that annoying face-pulling girl.)

Dad says when the cousins come over we might go out to eat for a change...

"As a special treat." (YEAH!)

"There's a new place in town that's just opened up, which would be good for the cousins too," he adds.

"Why would it be good for the cousins?" I ask.

"It's all you can eat."

Sounds like my kind of restaurant.

Yum

DINNER
With the Cousins

Aunty Alice and Uncle Kevin are dropping the cousins off REALLY early this morning, so Mum and Dad are rushing around tidying the house up.

I'm trying to watch some TV before they arrive, but Mum keeps puffing up cushions and vacuuming around me, which is annoying.

When they all arrive, Aunty Alice tells Mum, "The house looks S⃝O tidy, I hope you didn't clean especially for us!"

And Mum says, "NO, of course not, we always have a tidy at the weekend."

(Which is news to me.)

 I take the cousins and show them my new doodle wall. They like it a LOT.
"Here, have a draw if you want," I say.

"What shall we draw?" they ask.

So I suggest they could draw a **MONSTER** or maybe some funny pictures of their family. "I do it all the time."

Their doodles don't go down too well with Aunty Alice or Uncle Kevin when they come up to say goodbye. As they're leaving, Dad tells Uncle Kevin, "You have to admit, it was a good likeness, Kevin."

(It was.)

I ask the cousins if they fancy a snack? (Like I don't know the answer already.) 🙂

We go down to the kitchen to see what there is to eat. "Oh look," I say, pretending to be surprised. "We have bananas ... lots of them, help yourselves."

Luckily for me, they do, which helps the numbers go down.

I'm getting a bit fed up of bananas.

Dad's asking them about school and what are they up to and even worse, "What kind of music do you like, then, lads?" Which is embarrassing, especially as he's never heard of ANYONE they say.

Worse still, Mum wants to know if we want to make biscuits?

BISCuITS!

"**M**UM! They won't want to make biscuits ... you don't, do you?"

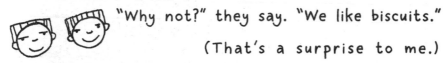 "Why not?" they say. "We like biscuits."

(That's a surprise to me.)

Mum gets out all the ingredients and we make biscuits. We make a bit of a mess too, but I get away with leaving it because the cousins are here.

Delia has suddenly appeared and is hovering around, trying to help herself to one of our freshly cooked biscuits. So I tell her...

"If you want a biscuit, you need to SAY, '**Please** may I have a biscuit, my lovely brother, **Tom**?' and I might let you have one."

The rest of the day I keep the cousins busy by watching (non-scary) films.

We go next door and hang out with Derek while taking Rooster for a walk. Which is fun.

Derek says, "Your cousins are very tall, aren't they."

"Do you think so?" I say as we walk behind them.

GOING OUT

We're getting ready to go out to eat when Dad does his usual thing of rushing round the house turning off all the plugs. We're all sitting in the car waiting to go when he remembers one he's missed. Mum says, "Come ON, Frank, we'll be late!"

I want him to hurry up because I'm a bit squashed in the car.

When we get to the restaurant, it's REALLY busy, with loads of families all piling their plates up with food. We're shown to a table and told that depending on what size plate we have, that's how much it costs to eat.

ALL YOU CAN EAT

Dad says we can all have a MEDIUM-sized plate. "That's more than enough, I think."

small medium large

There's SO much food to choose from I don't know where to start!

The cousins seem to know what to do.

pasta

I can't help thinking I've been here before, even though I know I haven't.
I go and help myself to a really nice dinner of everything I love.

Mum tries to add some extra vegetables to my plate, which makes some of my food spill over on to the table. She says, "Never mind ... whoops!

whoops

I 'll ask the waitress to clear it up."

groan

waitress

 But the waitress we've got doesn't
want to come over.

She even turns her back on Mum and tries
to ignore her. Mum has to find someone else
to help instead.

Mum says, "CHARMING. I'm not leaving
a tip for her!"

Dad's plate isn't too bad. He reminds Mum
about his body being a temple again, which
makes both of us roll our eyes.

But the cousins' plates are something else.

They spend **AGES** stacking them up as carefully as they can, with as much food as possible. They're balanced like a tall tower. If someone hadn't accidentally knocked into them, they would have made it to the table, too.

But they didn't.

AGH!
We watched THREE huge mountains of food collapse over the floor, tables and splatter some of the other diners too. Who weren't very happy.

The whole of the restaurant was staring at the food and us. It was REALLY embarrassing. Especially for one waitress who was sent over to help clean up the mess ...

... at least we all know where Delia works **nOW**. And where I'd seen those hats before! (Mum decided to leave her a tip after all.)

When Delia got home later I told her
the food was very nice just before she
SLAMMED her bedroom door.

In the morning she was still **MAD**.

"This WHOLE family is a NIGHTMARE. And you WONDER WHY I didn't want to tell you where I worked!"

She's got a point. It was quite funny, though. The cousins don't help much by reliving the whole story for Aunty Alice when she comes to pick them up. She says they had a nice weekend but Uncle Kevin's golf swing was a bit crooked so he's recovering at home with a cricked neck.

sore neck ←

W hen I got home from school today, THIS letter was waiting for me.

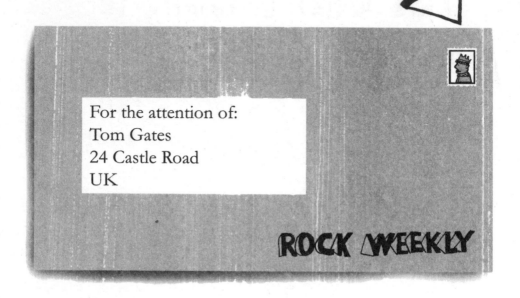

For the attention of:
Tom Gates
24 Castle Road
UK

ROCK WEEKLY

Not just any old letter – it's from
ROCK WEEKLY magazine.
I know this is going to sound really WEIRD,
but I take back EVERYTHING I've ever said
that was BAD about having a grumpy sister.

I can honestly say that RIGHT now (it might change later) my sister DELIA is the best sister in the whole wide world EVER. I actually want to go and HUG her and say
thank you - thank you - thank you - to her for being so brilliant and

ABSOLUTELY FANTASTIC

(at most things).

Because the letter from **ROCK WEEKLY** magazine says that I've only gone and WON the T-shirt design competition!

So NOW **DUDE3** will be printing and WEARING my design. I get some FREE T-shirts too.

I am so EXCITED I can hardly breathe.

I've been leaping round the room and have already run round to tell Derek, who's just as excited as I am.

So the REASON I have to be nice to Delia

(for as long as I possibly can)

is because she found my design that I completely forgot to post and posted it for me. My entry got there in time for the deadline.

I'm SO HAPPY!

Delia is a little uncomfortable with me being so nice to her.

"It feels odd. Back off, will you?" she tells me when I bring her a cup of tea.

The only thing Delia really wants from me is:

1. I (or any family member) am not allowed to come to THAT restaurant again when she's there. (Fine by me.)

2. One of my T-shirts when I get them.
   (No problem.)
3. To stay out of her room. (OK, will do.)
4. To stop writing stupid songs about her.
   (Even though they're not stupid.)

What have you put in it?

Mum and Dad say how nice it is to see us
getting along so well.
And Delia says, "Don't worry, it won't last."
                (Which is probably true.)
                        The end.

Different uses for Delia's hat

All you can READ

The next Tom Gates book is out September 2013...

Fancy doing a doodle?

Try out the Tom Gates DOODLE GAME!

Go to: www.scholastic.co.uk/tomgatesdoodles

http://tomgatesworld.blogspot.co.uk/

How to do a BANANA doodle

Take a banana and a cocktail stick (mind the sharp end).

Carefully push the stick into the banana skin – not too deeply.

Where you make a hole it will turn black. You can do a doodle like this quite quickly.

Don't leave the banana too long before you eat it, as the doodle will go darker and darker (then go mouldy – yuck).

Did you find all the
monsters?

I am ABSOLUTELY **F**ANTASTIC
(at SOME things).

LIKE drawing **MONSTERS**.

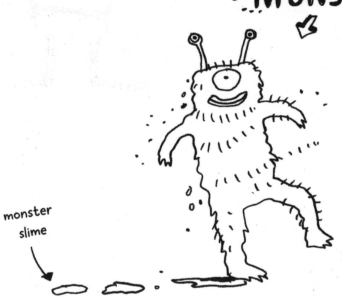

monster
slime

BUT I am NOT so good at drawing
REAL hands

or feet (which are tricky).
Here's a picture of Marcus with

MONSTER hands and duck feet instead.

I'd forgotten about the new neighbours until ...

(To be continued...)

Have You Got ALL the TOM GATES books yet?

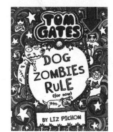

ALL NEW COVERS!

www.scholastic.co.uk/tomgatesworld